FARAWAY
AND
FOREVER

FARAWAY AND FOREVER

MORE STORIES

NANCY JOIE WILKIE

SHE WRITES PRESS

Published 2023
Printed in the United States of America
Print ISBN: 978-1-64742-454-1
E-ISBN: 978-1-64742-455-8
Library of Congress Control Number: 2022923356

For information, address:
She Writes Press
1569 Solano Ave #546
Berkeley, CA 94707

Interior Design by Tabitha Lahr

She Writes Press is a division of SparkPoint Studio, LLC.

*Thank you so much
to my wonderful editor—
Rebecca Carroll Christensen.*

*And thank you
to all of my beta readers—
John Eggers, Patrick Twomey,
Rev. Emily Hart, Peter Heuberger,
Carol Abrahams, and Nancy Cox.*

*And last, thank you, Dad, for your gift
of the place in Bethany Beach, DE.
It is a wonderful place to write.
"A special gift for a special person."*

CONTENTS

ONCE UPON A HELIX

(The Firmament and the Filament)

. . . .

ONE

THE SCREEN OF THE VISIPHONE suddenly popped on and the crackle of static filled the chill dry air. Pale light from the forming image illuminated the sparsely decorated hotel room. It was still dark outside, but that didn't mean anything in lower Manhattan. Much to the consternation of the room's temporary occupant, the city never slept.

"Sorry to wake you, sir, but something rather significant has happened," said a young man of Indian descent.

Gunther Trent was never very good at waking up, especially when he had just gone to sleep. It reminded him of the countless mornings when he had pulled himself out of bed during college for 8:00 a.m. classes. He thought it ironic he wound up teaching some of those very same classes years later and hated getting up early even more. Acquaintances could always tell when he had not gotten his seven hours of rest the night before. And to be interrupted tonight of all nights when he had to make a big pitch in the morning to some potential corporate backers. *Damned hotel pillows*, he thought as he rolled over to activate the terminal.

"Yes, Jai. What's so darn important you had to wake me up? Don't you know what time it is?"

Jai ignored his former mentor's abrupt response, squared his shoulders, and braced himself for the flood of questions to follow. An assertive stance always worked best, even though his self-confidence took a hit. Testing the employment waters outside the known bounds of his current position came to mind once again, but at least he knew where he stood with Trent. Wouldn't a different boss be just as demanding? *The evil of two lessers*, he thought.

"We've detected a signal. Twenty minutes ago. It's repeating."

Trent stumbled out of his warm bed, reached for his robe, and tied it securely around his waist, "What? Are you sure?" His tall, imposing figure bent over the computer monitor, leaning on his left arm for support.

"Yes, I'm sure. I checked it three times. We've received the exact same set of signals almost a dozen times. I wanted to be sure before I called."

"Are you recording it?"

"Yes, sir."

"You're doing fine, son. What frequency did it come in on?" asked Trent eagerly.

"Sixteen hundred sixty-two megahertz."

"Excellent! The hydroxyl line. The early researchers predicted it would be one of the magic frequencies, and they were right! Damn smart of these aliens to use a fingerprint of the water molecule as the frequency."

"One other thing, sir, the signal is very strong. Much stronger than if extraterrestrials received some of our television transmissions at the same distance. Much stronger than if someone sent it out in all directions simultaneously from their transmitter. One might conclude it is directed at us, at Earth, or at least our solar system."

"Can you tell what it says?" Trent asked impatiently.

"No, sir."

"No, of course, you can't. Sorry, I'm a little excited here. Can you show me the signal pattern of the message?"

The visiphone made a subtle crackling noise as the view switched from Jai's face to a series of wave patterns. "Sure enough, that's not background noise. After all these years, there it is! The first evidence humanity is not alone in the universe reduced to a series of wave patterns on a computer screen! Fantastic!"

Four distinct sharp peaks stood out in the first part of the message. The second, third, and fourth spikes appeared to be increasing multiples of the first. The set of four signals then repeated twice. A long stream of one hundred or so peaks with intensities identical to the first one followed an even longer stretch of thousands of spikes dominated by random arrangements of the first four signals. Every eighth pulse in this part of the message had a different intensity. Then the original four peaks repeated two more times before a very long sequence of spikes with what appeared to be widely varying strengths. One thing was clear, whoever sent the message must have wanted to make sure anyone listening would notice it above the background noise of the cosmos. The strong, sharp pulses had found their way across light-years of space and into the impressive array of radio telescopes situated around the globe.

"Where's it coming from?"

"I'm not sure yet. Looks like somewhere in the southern part of Ursa Major. I'm working on it." Jai hated not having the answer Trent wanted. "What should I do now, sir?"

"First of all, don't say a word to anyone! Got it? No one, at least not until I get back out there, and we can verify this thing!" Trent fired back.

"But what about the scientific protocol we're supposed to follow if we pick up a signal?"

"To hell with it right now. We've got too much riding on this. The existence of the program may rest on how we handle this. They'll be plenty of time to communicate our findings to the appropriate authorities if this is a real live catch."

"But what about the tracking stations?"

"You're a worrywart, son. With everyone trying to pull our plug, I doubt anyone else will be listening. If anyone does call, tell them it's a test, or you've determined it's someone's idea of a practical joke. If they're really insistent, tell them I'll get back to them when I return. I'm going to take a quick shower, pack, and be on the first shuttle back to LA. To hell with all these self-important business types and their funds! If this is the real thing, I won't need to beg for handouts any more to keep our ears on!"

As the screen went dead, Trent quickly scrolled through the contact information on his smart phone, looking for the number of Dr. Benjamin Summers. He keyed in the correct number. Seconds later, a gray-haired gentleman appeared on the visiphone screen.

"Trent? Gunther Trent? Is that you? What the hell do you want in the middle of the night? You're damned lucky I stay up so late. You know we have a meeting with the Board of Directors in the morning. Shouldn't you be getting your beauty sleep?"

"That's exactly why I'm calling, Ben. Something's come up. I need to cancel this morning's meeting. I've got to fly back to the West Coast as soon as I can get myself to the airport."

"But what about the funds? You've been begging me for weeks to set up this meeting with my buddies in the corporate world so you can try to get them to sponsor the SETI Institute. With the fate of the institute hanging in the balance, what could possibly be more important than . . . hey, wait a minute . . . you didn't stumble upon something, did you?"

"Look, Ben, you and I go way back. You've got to trust me on this one. I know I wanted this meeting, but I need to get back out West immediately. Can't you just put them off for another couple of days? Please?"

"There are times, Trent, when I question my own sanity for hanging around the likes of you. If I didn't believe in the cause," Ben looked off to his left as if to check something on his desk. "All right. As soon as the sun rises, I'll make the necessary calls. At least I have the decency to let my acquaintances sleep uninterrupted through the night."

"Thank you, Ben. If this pans out, you won't need to apologize."

"Hey, wait a minute! What are you talking about? Trent. Trent! Answer me!"

Trent, determined not to say anything more before he got out of New York, let the line go dead. He flipped on the lights, found his boarding pass, and called the shuttle service to reschedule his flight. There was just enough time to clean up and get to the airport.

The cold floor tiles greeted his bare feet as he entered the bathroom. Standing in front of the small mirror above the oval sink, he surveyed his stubble-covered face. There were the few gray hairs sneaking up his temples, but at least he wasn't losing his hair like so many of his peers. He felt good about that.

What if this signal is real?

He stood there for a long time, the can of shaving cream in his right hand, thinking about the possibility. The SETI Institute and the trillion-channel extraterrestrial array it used was dying and, along with it, his professional career. He knew that. Sooner or later, he would have to face up to that fact. Had Lady Luck finally chosen to shine upon him?

Jai says the signal is strong.

More than a century earlier, scientists discovered that cosmic background noise would eventually overwhelm radio and television signals sent from Earth into space by the time they reached the nearest stars. They would be virtually undetectable at greater distances unless the cosmic listener had an incredibly sophisticated receiver. Had humans ever wanted to, though, they could have increased the likelihood of an extraterrestrial race detecting a signal from Earth by directing an intense beam at a specific target. But Earth had quite purposefully not sent any strong signals out to nearby stars. Conversely, any strong signal received by humans had to mean someone must be sending a message specifically for humans to hear.

Great minds who had thought through why someone would want to transmit a message across the cosmos concluded it was done either passively or intentionally. A passive communication might be their equivalent of a simple "hello" or "we have green skin and two heads." But a message sent intentionally would likely be either an invitation or a warning. If such a signal was ever received, Trent prayed it would be a call from neighbors wanting to establish a peaceful co-existence with their interstellar neighbors. He couldn't quite conceive why someone would send a warning or, if they did, what it might say. But any warning, Trent figured, would probably be something to take seriously.

He recounted the signal patterns. There were the sets of four distinct peaks dominating the message. That puzzled him. What was the purpose of those? They appeared periodically throughout the message as if they were some sort of cosmic commas. Maybe they were the key to translating the signals into something meaningful. Did the senders of this message anticipate whoever received it would need a means to decipher the transmission? Of course, they did. But would they know who might receive the message? Assuming the signal was aimed at Earth, did they know something of Earth and, therefore, tailor their message with Earth in mind?

Trent made a mental note to double-check everything Jai had done to screen out the possibility the military, NASA, or a commercial communications satellite generated the message. And better check the computer programs constantly scrutinizing each of the trillion channels, too. Nothing can be left up to chance. If this was real, it would become the most analyzed piece of electronic data in history.

He took a deep breath and began applying the shaving cream in a calculated manner. First the cheeks, then the chin, the bottom of his angular jaw, his neck, and last the space between his nose and upper lip. There was a finely-tuned sequence of applying shaving cream, developed over the years, if for no other reason than to combat the sheer drudgery of shaving. And the shaving followed the same sequence. So predictable.

This can't be happening to me. Something must be wrong, he kept thinking.

Trent had something of a reputation in the world of astronomy as the last holdout for keeping the search for extraterrestrial intelligence and the SETI Institute alive. His colleagues, if not the entire population of the civilized world, had long since given up on the idea Earth might one day receive a message from an extraterrestrial intelligence. Isn't one hundred years of listening enough time to convince the scientific community there is no one else in the gigantic universe but us insignificant humans?

Early in his training to be a radio astronomer, Trent had studied the history of the SETI Institute and admired the vision driving its early pioneers to establish a systematic survey for signals from space. Support for such a program came from mostly ordinary people hungering for some evidence extraterrestrial life existed. UFO sightings became a common occurrence. Television, films, and magazines of the time saturated an eager public with stories claiming aliens had crash-landed and the government held their bodies and spaceship at a secret location.

The original SETI equipment was launched in the 1960s. By the beginning of the 1980s, technological advances helped establish the million-channel Project META. But it took another fifteen years to activate a third-generation radio telescope array, and only then did the

16

search gain any chance of succeeding. Computer capability allowed astronomers to simultaneously monitor one billion channels, process billions of operations per second, and analyze the data in a reasonable amount of time. Hopes soared when conclusive proof that microscopic organisms had evolved on Mars. Fundraising was like collecting rain in a bucket.

Then came nearly one hundred years of fruitless listening. People eventually realized it wasn't an issue of whether life existed out in the stars so much as it was a question of when extraterrestrial life had existed or would exist. After all, it wasn't only a three-dimensional search to find a star having just the right-sized planet with just the right set of biochemicals at just the right distance from its sun to support life. It was also a search of when did or when will some nearby magic planet give rise to life. Astronomers estimated the Milky Way galaxy to be ten billion years old, the sun four billion years old. If their calculations were correct, the sun would go on burning for another five billion years or so. Assuming all of our stellar neighbors had similar life spans, that was an awful lot of past and an awful lot of future and very little present. It was unlikely humankind would find any stellar neighbors.

"Oh, to have been a planetary scientist in those days," sighed Trent. "Back when it meant something to be a pioneer." Trent smiled as he remembered reading about the first director of SETI and his gift for making the public want to invest in science, a talent any businessman would envy.

His being in charge of the project was not because Trent was brilliant or a good fundraiser. No, he was in charge because no one else would take the job. All of his predecessors and associates had long since gone out into academia, the government, or the private sector and found themselves high-profile, high-paying positions. His title of Project Director wasn't something to be proud of in professional circles anymore but was almost something of which to be ashamed.

The belief there would be an opportunity to do research and to catch up on writing was what attracted Trent to the job. Had he known most of his time would be spent raising funds to keep the project alive, he might have thought twice before accepting the position. He hated having to be a salesman, constantly trying to convince potential private or corporate backers the project represented the chance to fulfill one of humanity's oldest dreams. He didn't want the dream to die. "Just a little longer," he kept telling people. "Give it another chance."

But the economic conditions of the twenty-first century had not been kind to the program. Circumstances in society became more challenging. Unemployment went up. Inflation went up. The federal government, strapped by the massive debt it had incurred during the second half of the twentieth century, had no choice but to cut back on unnecessary programs. And even though the government did not fund the SETI Institute, discretionary spending by corporations and private organizations began to dwindle because the program wasn't producing anything. More than once, it had been in danger of termination. But each time, one of Trent's predecessors managed to avoid being shut down by compromising away some less critical aspect of the project. Recently though, funds were threatened again. Unfortunately, Trent had nothing left to give up except the barest essentials.

He was alone, the last scientist to devote his entire time and attention to the project, the last pillar holding up a fantastic dream. He had given up everything to keep it going. His professional reputation was that of a fool, someone who could not let go of the past. His personal life had taken its toll, as well. After years of working late into the night one too many times, his wife divorced him and headed off for greener pastures. If this were the real thing, he had paid a dear price for it. Perhaps it would be worth it.

Maybe I'm crazy, thought Trent. He finished shaving, dialed room service, and ordered a light breakfast. While he waited, he put on his traditional uniform of smartly pressed khaki pants, a white button-down Oxford cloth shirt, a blue crewneck sweater, and a pair of well-polished loafers. He checked himself in the mirror.

Breakfast arrived, and the welcome smell of strong coffee invigorated him. Trent sat down at the round table in front of the window and watched New York City wake up.

What if it was real? What would he do? No, he knew what he was going to do. And this discovery would help him recapture the magic that had first drawn him into the field of astronomy. Wonder and excitement stirred within him. Yes, this could be his big break. But there were no guarantees. The moment his findings were announced, his life would change. People would want his time, perhaps take his work and turn it into theirs or, worse yet, attempt to make the discovery something it wasn't. He couldn't control the outcome. In all likelihood, it would control him. Yet the gamble might be worth it. The parameters of his current life would change, to be sure. The thought left a bad taste in his mouth. He lifted his coffee cup, made a silent toast to himself, and drained it.

Something kept nagging him as he packed his overnight bag. What key had the alien sender used to help its listener understand the signal pattern? Out of habit, he checked the room one final time, and closed the door carefully so as not to wake any of his fellow hotel guests. As the door shut behind him, he thought about where this day might take him. By ten, he was at the airport and waiting for the boarding call.

TWO

CATHERINE ARKETTE SURVEYED herself in the full-length mirror hanging on the backside of her bedroom door, scrutinizing her appearance with her usual critical eye. She didn't think of herself as beautiful, but she knew others considered her attractive, especially her male coworkers and associates. Still, she wanted to look her very best with so many of her high-profile peers present at the Human Genome Society Annual Awards Ceremony. Anybody, assuming they were still living, who had made any contribution to the advancement of humankind's understanding of human genetics, would be there. She just wished the meeting wasn't so far away. Even with all of the recent innovations in aeronautical engineering and the new near-space shuttles, she disliked flying with a passion. To travel all the way across the country for a scientific meeting? Was it really worth it?

As Catherine stood there judging her attire, someone who didn't know her would think she was the picture of perfection. She wore a long red dress with a simple pattern of small white polka dots. A white linen blazer covered her bare arms, protecting them from the air conditioning that would, no doubt, make its presence known on the near-space flight. And there was the ever-present hint of curls in her shoulder-length sandy blonde hair.

Beneath such brilliantly balanced attire, though, there was a host of uncertainties. Catherine did not possess the level of self-confidence one would naturally assume. She was a charming, caring individual, full of smiles, very professional at work, and very polite in her social interactions with friends and family, to be sure. And she did have a wide variety of interests, from music and water sports to the arts. But none of that could quite cover up the anxiety she felt around other people. The isolation of the laboratory beckoned to her when she first became a graduate student. But as her career skyrocketed, her success brought her more and more professional and social obligations. So much so that lately she had almost forgotten about one of the reasons she became a scientist.

But social isolation was not the only incentive for entering science. Catherine also had a passion for solving puzzles and trying to find the magic key which would unlock the secrets of the living cell, finally allowing humanity to devise a cure for cancer. So many people had come so close during the last decade. All the pieces were there. Medicine was just waiting for some bright scientist to put them together in the right way. It had to happen soon.

The purpose of the Human Genome Project was to collect the information necessary to understand and ultimately find cures for not only cancer, but all other genetically-based diseases. Its primary goal was the sequencing and mapping of all three billion base pairs of the human genome. And that it did by the end of the first decade of the new millennium. The effort had been overwhelming and demanded new technologies for handling and storing DNA samples, DNA sequencing, and the analysis of massive amounts of information, all being developed simultaneously. The ingenuity of humankind had not let the project down.

The project's founders had been bright enough to realize there would be other pieces required to unlock the secrets stored away in the human cell once mapping and sequencing were complete. Their foresight and the open-ended approach to the project helped assure entire chromosome complements of half a dozen other species were investigated, as well. The hope was to discover what gave other animals an increased resistance to diseases fatal to humans.

But ethical overtones arose ever since man first started dissecting human chromosomes. Throughout the long years of the project, a small percentage of the budget dealt with the ethical issues arising from the ever-increasing number of scientific discoveries. Early on, the public panicked that some genetically-altered mutant might escape into the environment and spread new diseases. And they feared the ability to manipulate human genes would make shopping for the perfect baby commonplace. Some people even dreaded that science would disassemble the miracle of life into a set of chemical reactions, downgrading the wonder of God's creation. They equated humankind's search to understand the mechanics of life as taking a bite of fruit from Eden's Tree of Knowledge.

In the end, the potential benefits to humankind won out. When the world saw young children with incurable illnesses being healed, the furor died down, and biochemists were given greater freedom to experiment. Now all the arm twisting, fundraising, planning, and a century of tedious work was over. The project was on the verge of giving the medical community the ammunition it had dreamed of for hundreds of years. The only significant ethical question remaining was, what would be the consequences of radically reducing the number of sick people in the world?

The doorbell rang three times without interruption and snapped Catherine out of her morning reverie. Without bothering to check through the peephole, she opened the door and walked away from it all in one motion. "Hello, neighbor," trailed her voice as she returned to the living room.

"Good morning, Cat. Are you ready for some breakfast?"

"All set. Got my bag, my briefcase, and my plane ticket."

"My, don't we look smart today."

"Oh, come on, Lizzie. You know I've got to go to LA today."

"Oh, that's right," said Lizzie in a mocking tone. "It must be wonderful to be a famous scientist off to receive another award, rub elbows with all the great minds of the world, and talk about all sorts of cerebral things. Me, I'll just go off to my menial job in the accounting department of a large metropolitan corporation."

"Stop it! You have a lot going for you! You have looks, you have talent, and you have a wonderful boyfriend." Catherine purposefully communicated a certain amount of envy with her eyes to emphasize the word "wonderful."

"Don't flatter me. My skirts are too short, I wear too much makeup, take long lunch hours, and I'm late for work at least twice a week."

"And you have the most beautiful singing voice, and you're a really great best friend," continued Catherine as she juggled her bags and locked her apartment door simultaneously.

"Thanks."

They rode the elevator down to the apartment lobby together, walked out through the automatic doors and headed north several blocks to their favorite coffee shop. They found a table in the back corner. Catherine placed her briefcase on the extra chair and her carry-on bag on the floor.

"*Bon matin*, mademoiselle. What is it that you would like for your breakfast?" The same young French waiter made it a point to wait on the pair whenever they graced the café with their presence.

"I'll have a poppy seed bagel, a small glass of orange juice, and a mocha Java espresso," answered Catherine.

"And you, mademoiselle?"

"My usual, please." The usual meant coffee with six lumps of sugar and toast burnt around the edges.

The waiter scurried off to the kitchen. Lizzie cocked her head to the side to survey the clientele. "Still checking out potential members of the opposite sex, are we?" mused Catherine.

"And not finding any decent ones in here, except for our waiter friend. Oh, well. So tell me, are you all ready to let the scientific world in on your latest work?"

"Whatever are you talking about?" responded Catherine trying to look humble.

"Oh, come on. You know the biochemical-some-thing-or-other stuff you were so excited about a couple of nights ago. It had something to do with DNA, I think."

"Ugh! I can't stand it when lay people butcher perfectly good science!"

They both giggled like they were twenty years younger. The kitchen door burst open, and their server came in and set down all of the plates and cups, making certain he lingered just long enough to offer a polite remark or two.

Lizzie took a bite out of her toast with an audible crunch. "I know I kid you about being a science nerd and all that, but I want to tell you I actually enjoy learning from you. Whenever I explain any of this to the other girls in the office, they think I'm some sort of rocket scientist. The other day, someone was talking about an article in the paper having to do with some genetic whatchamacallit and I used your analogy about DNA resembling a ladder. You know, when you equate science to everyday things ordinary people can understand, it's really not so bad. I even remembered the part about there being only two kinds of rungs on the ladder." Lizzie beamed like a schoolgirl who had just come home with an "A" on her report card.

"I'm impressed! Tell me more about the rungs." Catherine sat and listened as if she were the schoolgirl's proud mother.

"Well, there are A–T rungs and C–G rungs. Don't ask me what the letters stand for. I keep track of which letters go with which because your initials are 'C' and 'A' and they don't go together," Lizzie said without finishing the thought. "And I think I finally understand the part where the rungs can be either A–T or T–A and C–G or G–C, so there are actually four choices. Then the ladder's twisted to resemble a spiral staircase. The rest of the stuff about the ladder unwinding itself and sending out messages to the cell to make copies I still don't get. I have to leave something for us for future lessons, don't I?"

"Wow! You really have been paying attention to me over the last several months, haven't you? That makes me feel good! It's so nice to have someone outside of work I can talk to about what I do, even if I have to teach high school biology first! I'll bet the guys in here wonder what two beautiful women like us are gossiping about. Wouldn't they be surprised?"

They both giggled again.

"Now, seriously, what about this week's meeting?" Lizzie pressed Catherine.

"To tell you the truth, Lizzie, I'm not ready to announce anything just yet. I need some more time to figure out the significance of what I've found. I know I talked about the importance of the finding, but I'm going to wait a bit longer."

"All right. You need to do whatever you think is best. I just don't want some hotshot *man* scientist to beat you to the punch."

"Always looking out for me, Lizzie. Thanks." Catherine looked up from the table and motioned over the waiter. "We'll take the check, please."

The two women pulled out their smart phones, typed in the correct amounts plus a generous tip, and got up to leave. "Au revoir, ladies. Hope you have a wonderful day. Come back soon," said the waiter with a wave.

Lizzie spun around and gave the young man a big wink. "Oh, you're bad. What would John say?" joked Catherine.

After leaving the grind and roar of the espresso machines behind, they walked to the curb. Lizzie gave Catherine a quick hug. "Good luck this week. I'll be anxious to hear how it all goes. And have a safe flight."

"Thanks," smiled Catherine. "Take good care of that man of yours. You don't know how lucky you are."

Catherine hailed a cab, opened the door, and threw in her bag and briefcase. She waved to Lizzie, climbed in the back seat, and settled herself. At first, the driver seemed intent on listening to unintelligible chatter coming from the knob-less radio. Then he finally asked in broken English, "Where you wanna go, lady?"

"LaGuardia, please," she answered politely. The meter started ticking.

Ignoring the eyes of the cab driver as he periodically scanned the rearview mirror, she looked out at the passing pedestrians, all in a hurry to get somewhere. In New York, it didn't matter what time it was. Someone was always going to work and someone coming home. The crowded thoroughfares of the city were somehow exhilarating. It seemed amazing one could be out in the middle of such pandemonium, feeling the comfort of not being alone, but yet still not have to engage in any social interaction. Maybe that's what she liked about it. Being with people, lots of people, but not having to talk to them or have any connection with them. *What a perfect combination*, she thought, as the cab worked its way from the high rises to the airport through rush hour traffic.

"Hey, you're that famous science lady I saw in a magazine a couple of weeks ago, aren't you?" The cabby's eyes sought to hold hers as Catherine looked up.

"If you're referring to the special report on the Human Genome Project in *New Earth News*, yes, I am."

"Ya, ya. But I don't understand all the fancy talk about genes and chromo-things."

Catherine suspected he didn't really care much about science and wasn't paying attention to his driving, either.

The cab swerved suddenly to the right to avoid hitting another car.

"Um, mister," began Catherine in a concerned tone.

"Did you see that idiot's driving? He nearly ran me off the road! Damn it! I hate stupid drivers."

Several minutes later, he appeared to have calmed down. Then a loud blast of a truck's horn in front of them caused her to look forward again. The honking was, no doubt, directed at the cab driver. She didn't quite know what to do about the situation, so she decided to ignore him, hoping he would lose interest and get her to the airport in one piece.

Thirty minutes later, the cab pulled up to the correct terminal. Catherine handed the driver a bill, not expecting any change. She opened the door and placed her things on the curb. "Thanks, lady," he said as his eyes followed her out the door.

She picked up her baggage, walked into the airport terminal, greeted the woman at the ticket counter with a brief smile, and headed down the concourse toward her gate. As she boarded the shuttle, she couldn't help wondering if she was doing the right thing by keeping the lid on her discovery for a bit longer.

THREE

SHORTLY AFTER 11:00 A.M., Trent boarded the near-space shuttle, found his seat next to the window, and stuffed himself into space designed to accommodate an average-sized man. Because he was tall, his knees came up to the level of the tray in front of him. He didn't look forward to several hours of discomfort.

The orange seat covers nauseated him. He wished the designers had picked a different color, something a little bit more aesthetically pleasing, perhaps a color that didn't remind him of why air sickness bags were included in the pouches behind every seat. The designers must have gotten a bargain on the color, Trent concluded.

He counted backward to figure the time on the West Coast. "Damn, I hate changing time zones," he grumbled.

As he puttered with the miniature buttons on his phone, a rather attractive woman stopped next to the adjacent seat. She looked up at the numbers printed on the overhead baggage compartments. After looking back down at her ticket, she sat down next to Trent and began to make herself comfortable.

At first glance, Trent judged the woman to be some sort of professional, perhaps a salesperson or a marketing executive. Her neat appearance suggested she was very conscious of how she came across with others. As he watched her open her briefcase to get out something to read, he could see she was also very organized, right down to having sharp pencils with new erasers available should she need them. Usually, he hated sitting next to anyone on long flights, but maybe this seemingly put-together woman could be the exception.

Trent noticed he was not the only one performing surveillance. The woman to his right took quick glances in his direction. Perhaps she might be open to chatting with him.

The near-space liner rolled down the runway and quickly left the ground. The tug of gravity pulled everyone a little deeper into their seats. Trent watched the cloud layers come and go as they climbed higher and higher, just beyond the uppermost parts of the atmosphere. It took little more than ten minutes for the shuttle to level its trajectory.

"The captain has just turned off the seat belt sign, and you are free to move about the cabin. We do ask, however, if you are seated, please keep your seat belt fastened," came the sultry voice of the flight attendant. "Have a pleasant flight."

Trent couldn't help but watch his seatmate out of the corner of his eye. As he sneaked a couple of quick glances, he thought she looked familiar. Typically, he didn't initiate conversations with total strangers, but the urge to engage this pleasant young woman started to get the better of him. Trent laughed at himself. *Ya, right. I'm going to start talking to a great-looking woman by saying, "Hey, don't I know you from somewhere?"*

But Trent knew he had seen her before and was frustrated he couldn't remember where. Resting his chin in the cradle between the thumb and index finger of his left hand, he finally decided it was her picture he had seen somewhere, perhaps in the newspaper or maybe in a scientific journal.

Then it struck him. *She was Catherine Arkette, an up-and-coming geneticist at Columbia University.* At least that's what he thought. And if it was her, then he was sitting next to a rising star in a field which had the whole world holding its collective breath, waiting for the final pieces of so many medical puzzles to fall into place. If not, he would have at least broken the ice and perhaps made this very attractive woman feel a bit special, even if for a moment. He started formulating a damage control plan.

Summoning up his courage, he turned to his seatmate. "Excuse me," Trent paused for a moment, still uncertain whether he should take the chance and embarrass himself. It must be her, he told himself again.

"Are you Catherine Arkette? Dr. Catherine Arkette?"

Trent thought the woman looked surprised at this query. *If it really was her, maybe she wasn't used to having total strangers recognizing her. But then again, if it was her, she was a fixture in her realm of scientific associates.*

"Yes," she said as she faced Trent and gave him a hint of a smile. "Yes, I am."

"Well, this is a pleasure, indeed," beamed Trent. "My name is Gunther Trent. I've read a lot of your work. I'm fascinated with the prospect of finding cures for so many diseases, all based on the fruits of the Human Genome Project."

Catherine let him go on without interruption.

"I've never pretended to understand all of the subtle nuances of the microscopic netherworld you molecular biologists live in, but the thing that always bothers me the most is trying to figure out which came first? DNA or proteins? How can proteins, which are coded for by a DNA molecule, manipulate the DNA from which they came, even to the point of rendering it inoperative?"

Catherine laughed and looked downward. Then she looked up again. "Well, it just so happens I read outside my field, too. You're that lone scientist still hanging on to the belief we should keep listening to the cosmos in hopes of tuning in to a celestial soap opera, aren't you?"

"You got me." Trent shifted in his seat so his knees pointed more in Catherine's direction. He was impressed she recognized him, a scientific outcast if there ever was one. "You know, I've read some of your work in popular journals. It's fascinating. Billions of base pairs all combining to give a set of instructions to itself. It is truly amazing," he said.

"And I've followed your attempts to keep radio telescopes listening for any hint there's someone besides us in this big ol' galaxy. I suppose I'm a minority these days, but I do believe there is intelligent life out there, somewhere. I just hope I live long enough to see the day when we find it."

A broad grin spread across the astronomer's face. "Is that so?" Trent checked to see if anyone was sitting in the seats in front of them or behind them. Empty. Good. "You seem like a sincere and trusting person. Can you keep a secret?"

"What do you mean?" Catherine tilted her head in a quizzical manner.

Trent lowered his voice. "I just might have what you've been waiting for."

"Really? Oh, then I can keep a secret!"

"Just this morning, my assistant picked up something definitely not of natural or terrestrial origin." Then Trent added, "At least we think that's the case."

"Wow. Do you know what it says?" asked Catherine eagerly.

"Nope." Trent shook his head from side to side. "That's why I'm on my way out West. I'm heading back to the observatory to take a look at it."

"That's amazing. You know, being a biochemist, I've often tried to imagine what other life forms might look like, what makes their biology tick. Can you imagine being the first to analyze the physiology and morphology of a genuine extraterrestrial life form? Your name would be forever etched in the archives of medical and biochemical journals." Catherine leaned over and placed her left hand on Trent's arm. "You wouldn't be looking for the services of a good biochemist, would you? I'd be more than happy to help. The heck with molecular biology!"

Catherine questioned Trent incessantly about the more detailed aspects of his research activities. It wasn't until she ran out of questions their discussion turned to Trent's current efforts to raise funds needed to keep the project going. The flight attendant interrupted them briefly to serve them their meal. As they finished, Catherine leaned back in her seat. "You know, it took humankind over twenty-five years to sequence the entire human genome and another seventy-five to figure out what all of those genes do. Promoter regions that turn on the genes, termination regions that turn off the genes, the random nonsense between the genes, and we've got almost every base pair in human DNA accounted for."

"You mean you gene jockeys have every single nucleotide pegged?"

"That's what everyone believes."

"Are you saying that's not so?"

"You were kind enough to trust me with an unannounced discovery of major importance. I'd like to return the favor. I'd like to tell you about Region X."

"I've never heard of Region X."

"Of course, you haven't. I just recently stumbled on it. As I reviewed the massive amount of information generated from decades of research, I found a section in the heart of the X chromosome not yet assigned a function. Every other region in all human chromosomes has been linked to some function, whether it's telling the cell to start making a protein, how to construct it, when to stop making it, or whether it's telling the cell nothing at all. Every region, except this region. And here's the totally bizarre part. The sequence of nucleotides in Region X is unique to the human X chromosome. It's not found anywhere else in all of the animal or plant kingdoms. Nothing even close."

"If I'm following you, don't many species have proteins or enzymes similar in function and, therefore, having comparable sequences in their respective DNA?"

"That's right. Generally speaking, a sequence for any given gene bears some resemblance to the sequence for the analogous protein in a related species. Granted, every species of life has not had its entire genome sequenced and mapped. But I have done computer searches looking for a match. Nothing. No sections of homology suggesting a similar sequence."

"Isn't that a bit odd?"

"Not entirely. But when it's combined with the fact the sequence contains a nucleotide never before seen anywhere in nature, including the rest of the human genome, then it becomes a bit odd. This discovery will be the first reported biological occurrence of this nucleotide. In other words, I've discovered a nucleotide previously unknown on the entire planet. I've isolated it and analyzed it and there's no mistaking it."

"What's the significance of a previously unreported nucleotide?"

"In and of itself, probably intellectual curiosity. But in the context of Region X, it's a piece of an extraordinary riddle. Most double-helical human DNA exists in the B form. This form is found most often within the cell nucleus. There are ten base pairs for each complete revolution of the helix. Under conditions of high humidity, DNA can change to the A form where there are eleven base pairs per turn. The C form only has 9.33 base pairs per turn. But no one has ever found any other double-helical form in nature until now. Region X exists in an eight base pair per turn configuration. This, I believe, is due to the presence of the novel nucleotide once every turn, once every eight nucleotide pairs."

"How do you explain all of this?"

"I can't. At least not by conventional means."

"What do you mean?"

"Forgive me, doctor. This might seem a bit, how shall we say, unscientific. Since I cannot find an analogous sequence anywhere in the entire animal or plant kingdoms, and since Region X exists in an eight base per revolution configuration, something never seen before, and since this previously unknown nucleotide cannot be found anywhere else on Earth, then I can only conclude the origin of both Region X and the nucleotide requires a different explanation."

"Are you suggesting what I think you are?" interrupted Trent.

"If you mean from outer space, I am. At first, I thought the concept of DNA dropping out of the sky to be a bit extreme. But then I recalled all the documented cases of meteorites determined to contain all sorts of bio-organic compounds. Think about the infamous Meteorite ALH84001 which carried the remains of primitive bacteria from Mars to Earth. Why not a complete sequence of DNA containing a unique nucleotide?"

"I suppose that's possible."

"Then I got to thinking again about how the sequence and its nucleotide appear only in humans. It seemed a bit too much to ask for some extraterrestrial DNA to survive countless years in the vacuum of space, survive entry through the atmosphere, and survive whatever conditions it found on Earth, only to selectively find its way into only one species, *Homo sapiens.*"

"I see your point."

"Based on the ubiquitous presence of Region X in the human population, it's now my personal and unprofessional belief that Region X, wherever it may have originated, was selectively introduced into the human genome at least one hundred thousand years ago."

"This is all very fascinating, but why are you telling me all of this?"

"I suppose because I haven't come up with a reasonable explanation, and I thought you of all people might have a sympathetic ear. I thought you might even use this as a means to justify the continuation of the SETI Institute. In fact, I even contemplated looking you up during my visit to LA."

Catherine bent over to pull out her briefcase from underneath the seat in front of her, opened it to retrieve a manila file folder, and then placed the briefcase back under the seat. Releasing the latch holding the tray in front of her, she unfolded a piece of chart paper, spreading it out on the tray for Trent to see.

"Is that an electropherogram of the DNA sequence for Region X?"

"Yes," said Catherine matter-of-factly.

"Amazing! Because it happens to bear an uncanny resemblance to the wave distribution pattern I saw on my computer screen this morning."

Catherine was stunned. "You're not kidding, are you?"

"No. My assistant showed me a printout this morning."

"I'm not sure I understand."

"Neither do I. But I'm heading back to LA as quickly as possible. I want to make an attempt at decoding the message before anyone else finds out about this. It's likely to turn the whole world upside down when word finally gets out."

"But what about Region X?"

Trent paused for a moment to collect his thoughts. "Catherine, you have shared with me your unpublished work, work which is incredibly significant. In turn, I have entrusted you with what will likely be the most crucial event in human history. Either one of these two events has uncalculated potential to affect humankind for a good long while. But if they are related in some way, and that appears to be a distinct possibility, matters become even more enormous."

They both sat for a moment, their heads spinning from the other's revelation. That these two scientific discoveries would be made at roughly the same time and be so inextricably linked to one another was astounding.

"It may be nothing at all," said Trent finally. "But I have a feeling we're on to something, something big. And if you're serious about your offer of professional assistance, I would gladly accept it."

Trent settled back into his seat and looked out his window at the gentle curvature of the earth.

"Of course, I'm interested!" said Catherine with a smile on her face.

FOUR

"A GAS GUZZLER! I DIDN'T KNOW people still drove these things. It must be worth a small fortune!"

"Yep. There's still something about rolling down the windows, turning up the radio, and pressing down on the accelerator that stirs one's blood," replied Trent. He was quietly impressed with himself at the thought of showing Catherine he wasn't just another stuffy middle-aged scientist.

"It's an old Chevy Nova," he continued. "I bought it from a little old lady about ten years ago. She said she only drove it to church on Sunday."

"You expect me to believe that story?"

"Actually, it's not far from the truth. The little old lady was my grandmother."

"Well, she had good taste in cars. And grandsons."

Trent registered Catherine's innocent little come-on and invited her to put her bag and briefcase in the back. "What do you say we go for a ride?"

They merged onto the expressway, full of early rush hour traffic. After a few minutes of trying to talk over the rush of air blasting through the open windows, they settled into their own thoughts. The previous three hours were a blur for Trent. So much to consider. The full weight of their respective discoveries began tugging at Trent's imagination. He remembered someone once saying that for one to be a really good scientist, the capacity to dream big dreams is essential.

Within thirty minutes, they were outside the LA city limits and making their way south along the Pacific coastline. Trent savored the California countryside with its arid and treeless terrain. He felt hints of damp air blowing in from the ocean, teasing the hills with its false prediction of rain.

As they turned eastward and began the gradual climb toward the mountains, the number of vehicles on the road finally petered out. Trent felt relief from concentrating so much on the driving and started to watch this impressive woman out of the corner of his eye. She seemed preoccupied or distracted, and Trent wondered what she was thinking. Was it a man? She wasn't wearing any sort of ring indicating a serious relationship. Yet he couldn't imagine someone with her charm being unattached. Maybe she was divorced.

What might it be like, he wondered, *to live in some fairytale world where Catherine and I make the two most significant discoveries of the century, begin a relationship, maybe even get married, and then live happily ever after.* He resisted the urge to say anything which might be construed as being the slightest bit unprofessional. Not now, it would only complicate things. But she was beautiful and intelligent.

A bit of a smile crossed his face as they continued snaking their way through the hills, through Pauma Valley, and toward Palomar Mountain State Park on the route nicknamed "Highway to the Stars." He switched on the car radio and found the all-news station, hoping to ease the uncomfortable silence settling in between them. Before heading southeast, they could see Oceanside and Carlsbad off in the distance. The late afternoon sun reflected off the ocean and painted patches of the surrounding landscape a bright gold.

"It's beautiful in its own strange way," mused Catherine.

"What do you mean?"

"You know how those towns seem dwarfed, almost insignificant to the greater world around them," she said softly.

But Trent ignored the view, keeping his eyes on the narrow road.

"Have you ever thought about what would happen if you made a big discovery? I mean the really big one?" asked Catherine. "You'd become world-famous. What would it be like?"

"Just this morning, as a matter of fact, just after I got word of the signal. How about you? What would it be like if you were the lucky one to find the cure for cancer?"

"Oh, I have. I must confess I'm almost afraid of it. I don't like being around lots of people. That's why I became a scientist. I like to be in my own little world, a world over which I can exert some degree of control. If something big happens with me, I'm not sure I'm going to handle it very well."

Do we really know what we're doing? Do we really appreciate what we're getting into? Trent asked himself these questions many times during the last few miles before they reached the top of the mountain.

By the time they reached the security gate at the observatory, the sun had started setting over the Pacific Ocean. There were very few sources of artificial light marking the entrance way and the parking lot. Trent explained that any unnecessary lighting detracted from the performances of the telescopes. The proximity detector accepted Trent's magnetically-coded security card and automatically opened the gate for them. He drove the last few hundred yards to the parking space labeled "Reserved for the Director," got out of the car, and walked around to the passenger side to open the door for Catherine. They followed the subdued amber glow of several small lights illuminating the path to the main Astrophysics Building and the stairway up to a set of double doors.

Once inside, they quickly crossed the lobby, climbed a flight of stairs to the second floor, and paused while Trent inserted his security card into the lock. As he opened the door to the laboratory, the sound of his former graduate student banging away on a computer keyboard could be heard quite plainly. The typing stopped for a moment. An anxious voice called out, "Dr. Trent? Is that you?"

"Hello, Jai," he said in a subdued voice. "It's me. I'm back. I'd like to introduce you to someone I met today on the flight out: Dr. Catherine Arkette. *The* Dr. Catherine Arkette."

Jai's jaw dropped as he stood to shake hands with Catherine. "It's a pleasure, ma'am. I've read a lot of your work."

"Is that all you astrophysicists do? Sit around and read the musings of a biochemist?"

Trent ignored the remark and headed for his desk and clicked on his computer terminal. Jai was caught off guard and didn't know what to say to their guest.

"Oh, I'm only kidding, Jai," Catherine finally said.

Jai seemed relieved and turned to give Trent his full attention. "A complete analysis of the message is on your desk, sir. I have now received the same message close to fifty times. And I think I've made some progress in locating the source of the signal. Plus 35.5 degrees by eleven hours. Right about where Lalande 21185 is located."

"Hmmm. If that's the source, then that's about 8.25 light-years from Earth. Not very far in terms of the cosmic big picture. Definitely a good candidate. We know it's got a solar system, just no gas giants, no Jupiter and Saturn. But there is at least one Earth or Mars-like planet there, maybe two, and they might just be orbiting in the Goldilocks Zone." Trent seemed to be pleased, and that made Jai feel good. "You've put in a long day, Jai. And you've done a fine job. Why don't you head home? Take a break. Get some sleep. You deserve it. You can finish up whatever you were doing tomorrow."

Jai, who had retreated to the far side of the room. "Um, okay, sir. Thanks."

Jai looked at Catherine, shrugged, and pulled off his white lab coat.

After the door closed behind Jai, Trent focused his attention on the signal readout, ignoring Catherine's gaze. He wondered what might lie behind those soft, wild eyes. It was difficult for him to imagine Catherine, with her sweet face and graceful figure, her light blonde hair, and her keen wit, had never married. *Perhaps this encounter might turn into something after all*, he thought. Then he quickly dismissed the notion.

"You know, you have Jai scared to death of you."

"Oh, for Pete's sake! It's good for the boy," Trent said stiffly.

"And why in heaven's name did you send him home when we might be on the verge of the greatest scientific breakthrough of our time?"

Trent frowned. "As much as I like Jai, I sent him home specifically *because* we might be on the verge of the greatest scientific breakthrough of our time. I think it's important to keep the details of the first message ever received from extraterrestrial beings as confidential as possible, at least for a while. Who the hell knows what it might say. It's better you and I be the only ones to read it before anyone else gets wind of it."

"I suppose you're right. But you still should be nicer to Jai. If I were twenty years younger, who knows?"

As much as Trent wanted to engage Catherine in a discussion about what physical attributes made a man attractive, he focused his attention on the chore of deciphering the message.

"Have you any ideas on where to start trying to figure out what the little green men might be trying to tell us?"

"Well, what distinctive characteristics does the message have?" Catherine sat on a backless wooden stool just off to the side of the bank of computer monitors, looking quite radiant, even after traveling for much of the day.

"There are sets of four peaks with relative signal strengths of one, two, three, and six recurring throughout the message and seem to break up the message into discreet sections."

"Yes, go on," Catherine said. She put one of her long index fingers to her chin as if to underscore the fact she was thinking.

"There are the sections themselves, their compositions, their relative lengths, the length of the whole message. Perhaps there's even some significance why the first section is first, the second section second, and so on. Might even be some importance to the apparently random portion of the signal between the more ordered sections," replied Trent.

"And what about the length of each repeat of the message? Is there anything unique about it?"

"Jai said he put the complete analysis here somewhere." He shuffled through the papers on his desk. "Ah, here it is."

Trent's eyes darted back and forth across the chart paper. He reached for a ruler and a calculator. "Yes. There does seem to be a very distinctive pattern to the ordered part of the message. If we assume the length of that portion to be an arbitrary unit of one, then there are 10.33 units of randomness between each repeat of what I believe to be the heart of the message."

"A 10.33:1 ratio. Is there anything significant about that?" probed Catherine.

"Not that I can tell," replied Trent. "Unless the senders are trying to tell us something about how many fingers they have," Trent said with a laugh. "Otherwise, I don't know."

"You might find this a bit odd, but that ratio says something to me. I told you on the plane an average double-helical DNA molecule twists around like a spiral staircase every ten base pairs or a helical pitch of 33.2 angstroms. When DNA is in that configuration, it has something known as a rise or the displacement along its axis of 3.32 angstroms, qualifying it as a 10:1 ratio. But you also might remember I told you Region X spirals around once every eight base pairs, equivalent to a helical pitch of thirty-one angstroms per revolution with a rise of three angstroms."

Catherine retrieved her smart phone from her purse and punched in the numbers thirty-one and three to the calculator app. She held up the answer for Trent, still sitting across the room.

"See? Exactly 10.33. Maybe the alien life is based on DNA having eight nucleotides per revolution. I could be completely off on this, but it seems to me DNA is certainly something significant, and it says something about the basis for life. Maybe they patterned the message after DNA because it spirals back on itself endlessly. Perhaps it would serve as a good model for a repetitive message."

Trent continued to silently search for some significant milestone in physics which might hold the key to the message.

"Now tell me more about these sections of the message," said Catherine after a minute of silence. "How many sections are there again and what are the characteristics of each section?"

Trent recounted what Jai had told him earlier in the day and described the repeating set of four distinct peaks, the stretch of one-hundred or so signals identical to the weakest of those four spikes, the thousand or so peaks containing a random arrangement of the four familiar peaks, broken up by a fifth unique spike every eight peaks, and the long, complicated final portion with signals of many different intensities.

Catherine slipped down off the stool and walked over to Trent's desk. She stood next to him and leaned over to study the readout.

"You know something? If I didn't know better, I'd say the whole structure of the message reminds me of mRNA."

"What?" Trent raised his head to gaze at Catherine, not quite comprehending where she was going with this analogy. "How can you draw any comparison between the message and nucleic acids. You can't seriously believe the whole message revolves around an mRNA molecule? Tell me, how would the four distinctive peaks recurring throughout the message relate to your model? I can't think of a damned thing. No significant scientific constants have a ratio of 10.33 combined with the number four. Why couldn't the senders have used some fundamental mathematical value or something more recognizable to an astronomer or physicist?"

Catherine stopped and closed her eyes for a moment and rubbed her temples with the ends of her delicate fingers. "Maybe that's it. We're approaching this through the eyes of an astronomer. Since you're an astronomer, you're looking out. I'm a biochemist. How about peering inward for a minute?" she suggested.

"Consider for a moment the analogy. It's perfect. Message RNA is the molecule carrying a reverse copy of the genetic code from the DNA in the cell nucleus out to the cytoplasm of the cell where it is used as the recipe for putting together amino acids in the right order to build a protein. Think about this message. It's carrying information outwards from a nucleus of sorts, from an alien civilization in another solar system to a distant planet where the information will be processed to build an idea of what these creatures are like. A perfect analogy."

Trent was silent. He redirected his attention back to the analysis, not thinking much of Catherine's biological approach to the problem. Unfortunately, he couldn't come up with anything better.

Catherine continued. "Then there's the issue of how the alien's message is constructed. First, there are the four strong peaks to which you referred. One hundred and forty-four spikes of equal intensity, all resembling the first pulse, follow. Then there's a repeat of the first four peaks succeeded by a long string of one thousand two hundred and twenty-eight signals and another four-peak repeat. After that, there's this extensive series of random spikes, all followed up by yet another four-peak repeat. I assume you remember something from your molecular biology class in college? An average mRNA molecule, or *messenger* RNA molecule," Catherine said, emphasizing the word, "has a sequence of about one-to-two hundred adenine residues at its three-prime end followed by up to two thousand nucleoside residues containing the instructions for one gene."

"I think you're a little off the track with this," chided Trent.

"You think so, huh? What about the four sharp peaks? What if they're somehow related to the nucleic acids found in RNA—adenine, cytosine, guanine, and uracil? What if the message makers are using the four peaks as a means for us to help decipher their transmission, establish a frame of reference?"

"I'm thinking this is getting just a bit crazy," replied Trent.

"Not at all. Remember a single strand of mRNA consists of a series of nucleotide strung together like a chain of beads. A sentence is nothing more than a strand of letters strung together in a similar manner. Over the years, theoreticians have attempted to build a mathematical model of molecular biology in order to help understand the incredibly complex logic Mother Nature devised. But cryptographers have also devised ways to encode information within a sequence of nucleic acids. Have you ever heard the term 'steganography'?"

Trent thought for a moment and then answered, "Isn't that the process of hiding information, images, or audio messages inside another piece of information?"

"Exactly. The term has been around for a good couple of hundred years. So, if the shorter ordered portion of this message is indeed some sort of nucleic acid sequence, it may well be that the much longer section in between has a message hidden inside it, perhaps an explanation for what the nucleic acid sequence is, why it's important, and why they are sending it to us."

"That's an awful lot of suppositions, dontcha think?" countered Trent.

"Well, maybe. Tell me again, how long was the more ordered section of the message? Didn't you say something like twelve hundred peaks?"

"That's right."

"It just so happens that the average length of an mRNA molecule is twelve hundred kilobases. And didn't you say that the random section of the message was about ten times longer?"

"Yep." Trent put down Jai's report and listened, truly listened, for the first time, to what his guest was proposing.

"So that means the in-between section of the message has about twelve thousand peaks. Making another huge assumption, if our interstellar neighbors chose the most prominent language on the planet for their message, which being English, they would know that the English language utilizes an alphabet consisting of twenty-six letters. If they devised a series of ciphers, where each cipher represented one letter, the question would be how many peaks would need to be in each cipher such that there are enough unique ciphers for twenty-six letters? At four peaks per letter, the length of the in-between section just might code for a reasonably-sized message."

Trent sat quietly, periodically shaking his head in

disbelief. Catherine had proposed what seemed to be a rational approach for how to decipher the message. "Okay. I give up. I would have never come up with any of this. If this works, you're a genius. Better that we take a crack at solving this puzzle now than have some yahoo do it after news of this hits the wires. And what might be your next step?"

Catherine pulled up a chair so she could see Trent's computer screen. "There are lots of software programs designed to detect the presence of steganography codes. Let's try one and see what happens. What do we have to lose? The trick will be finding the right decryption algorithm. I'm thinking that our interstellar neighbors would want us to break the code rather easily. So, we'll start with a few simple algorithms."

"I still think you're way out on a limb with all of this. How would the senders even know anything about DNA, its structure, or the letters of our alphabet? You're making a pretty big assumptions that they chose the English alphabet." Trent made several dismissive motions with his hands as he spoke.

"You better than anyone should know Earth has passively been sending television and other communications signals into outer space for almost 150 years. Any intelligent race could study the signals and know everything there is to know about our biology and our languages. They certainly could determine English is the dominant language on the planet and decide to use it. If Jai's right and the source is only 8.25 light-years away, then our friends would be only 8.25 years out of sync with our state of the art."

Trent did not offer up any more objections. After a pause Catherine continued. "So, in the absence of any other suggestions, what do you say?"

"All right. We might as well give it a whirl." Trent scratched his head, not knowing what to do next.

Catherine opened up a steganographic detection software program, entered the entire message, and then chose one of the simpler algorithms. Trent continued staring at the wave patterns from the alien message. "Do you have the printout with the sequence of Region X handy?"

Catherine stopped typing for a minute, retrieved the folded-up chart, and removed the paper clips as she handed it to Trent. She sat back down and continued working on finding an appropriate algorithm.

There was definitely an uncanny resemblance between patterns seen in the message and the sequence of Region X. Then Trent remembered Catherine mentioned a previously undiscovered nucleotide and that it was present every eight nucleotides throughout Region X. He looked at the second section of the message and saw that every eighth peak had an intensity which was different from the other four. *Could it be?* He said nothing to Catherine.

Trent heard the light clicking of Catherine's fingernails on the keyboard as he leaned back in his worn leather chair and closed his eyes. Why would there be a connection between these two seemingly unrelated items? Within minutes the sound of Catherine's voice broke into his internal quandary.

"It worked! Look, Trent! The third algorithm I tried did the trick! We have a translated message from someone out there!" The unoiled swivel of his chair protested as Trent leaned forward to inspect the computer screen. Catherine backed away from the instrument panel and stood up to make room for Trent to look.

Across the black computer screen came a series of fluorescent green words. The first four letters were, of course, already assumed to be A, C, G, and U. This was followed by one hundred and forty-four A's. What followed caused Catherine to gasp with obvious excitement.

"What's the matter? What is it?" asked Trent.

"It's the nucleotide sequence for Region X! I've been staring at it so much in the last few months, I could just about recite all twelve hundred base pairs by memory. It even has the odd-ball nucleotide at every eighth position! I don't get it, Trent. What's it mean?"

"I wish I knew, Catherine. You're the one proposing a connection between the message and mRNA. Little did you know it would also involve your Region X."

The computer finished displaying the sequence.

"I believe the answer to your question and the significance of the message is about to come up, assuming your algorithm worked."

Then, clear as the night sky powdered with the stars of the Milky Way, words from a message sent by beings on some unknown planet slowly crossed the screen.

Greetings, planet Earth. We are a race, not unlike yours. Our bodies are constructed out of the same biological building blocks, nucleic acids, and proteins. We intercepted transmissions from your planet many of your years ago. It took us much time, but we eventually learned your languages and began to study your society and your science. You appeared to be much as we were thousands of cycles past. Your world is full of war, disease, and hatred, just as ours once was. But your race is also advancing outward to the stars and inward to the secrets of life. We, too, advanced in this manner.

As we unraveled the last mysteries of our biology, we made a terrible discovery. We found hidden within the core of our genetic material a very peculiar sequence of molecules not native to our world. At first, we thought it just a mutation of our native nucleic acids. But upon further analysis, we realized the material was of extraterrestrial origin. And while we were thrilled at the possibility of life beyond our world, the true nature of what we uncovered became known to us. That is the reason we are sending this warning to your planet and your people.

Two thousand cycles ago, a violent race found their way to our world, just as they did yours. They placed sequences of alien nucleic acids into our genetic material, sequences that would not easily be found.

We, of course, knew nothing of the origin of this genetic material until it was too late. We did nothing with the discovery except catalog its existence. Many cycles later, their ships returned to fill our skies. Though they appeared hostile, they did not fire a single weapon at us. They simply stated we should surrender our planet to them, or they would unleash the second part of a deadly poison. At first, we resisted. Then they exposed millions of our people to a simple enzyme which found its way to that foreign piece of DNA present in every cell of our bodies. It chewed away our genetic material and killed millions of us within hours. We had no choice but to surrender to them.

It took hundreds of cycles for our scientists to secretly begin the purging process, freeing successive generations from the threat of the alien's biological weapon. Finally, when the invaders lost their hold on us, they left our planet.

If you find the alien nucleotide sequence we have included at the beginning of this message in your genome, then rest assured these hostile extraterrestrial beings will someday seek to control your planet as they once did ours. If we can make you aware of this danger before these invaders reach your planet, then you will stand a chance of avoiding the horrors that plagued our world. You must be convinced of the purpose of this genetic material and do whatever is necessary to extract it from your gene pool. If, upon arrival on your planet, these invaders become aware your species has discovered the existence of the foreign genetic material and removed it, then your peace will be secured. They will leave you and seek another world where their genetic weapon has taken root.

This will be your only message from us. It is unfortunate we cannot make contact with your society. After centuries of purging our gene pool of this poison, we fear recontamination by your species. We cannot take the risk. Your race will eventually conclude such a purging is the only way to rid yourselves of the potential enslavement by these aliens. When you have completed this task hundreds of years from now, then we will be ready to meet and to share the benefits such a relationship would bring. We will listen to our skies and wait for your message of healing.

Until then, our people wish your planet every success and look forward to the day when we can meet face-to-face. Farewell.

The message began repeating itself with the four-nucleotide marker. Trent and Catherine finished reading the translation. Trent reached over and switched off the screen. Catherine visibly shuddered. Neither spoke. They silently stared at each other for many long minutes. Trent fought down a sensation of panic, reminding himself of Catherine's presence. No sense in unnecessarily alarming her, too.

"I can't believe it. I didn't even consider the possibility the connection would lead to this. Humanity has spent the last thousand years pushing back the boundaries of the universe and exposing the secrets of how life itself works and, in one day, these two meet head-on . . . outer space and inner space . . . and, quite by chance, unlock the mystery of the other. And to what end?" Trent slammed his fist down on the desktop. "I'll tell you to what end, damn it! The entire population of our planet is at risk! The very existence of the human species! All because the two biggest, most long-awaited discoveries of the last millennium cancel each other out in one swift, decisive blow."

Catherine stood motionless across from Trent, her pale white hands neatly folded in front of her. She looked at Trent and said, "Restriction endonucleases."

"What did you say?" questioned Trent.

"The second half of the alien poison must be some kind of restriction endonuclease, an enzyme recognizing a certain sequence of DNA. In this case, Region X. And these enzymes cut DNA it in a very specific manner. Bacteria have these enzymes as a kind of defense against invading viruses. Each species has a different restriction enzyme which recognizes nucleic acid sequences present in attacking viruses, but not in their own genome. Kind of a neat trick nature created."

"All right. Let's imagine for a minute some master alien race planted this first part of a two-part poison at the core of our genome tens of thousands of years ago. How long would it take for it to spread to every man, woman, and child on the planet?"

"If you assume several thousand of our ancestors on each continent were genetically altered, assume the foreign DNA is somehow dominant rather than recessive, and assume an average of five generations per century for most of that time, then one hundred thousand years would be sufficient for Region X to find its way into the genome of every person on Earth."

"So, if the message is true, the bad aliens are patiently waiting in their little spaceships somewhere for their little mole to saturate the planet. Since they know the same set of statistics we do, they've probably already booked a return visit and plan to threaten our world with a deadly virus capable of eating human genes for breakfast. Have I accurately summed up the situation?"

"Trent, I think you're being just a bit dramatic."

"Am I? How would you describe it?"

"Okay, so it's a matter of semantics." Catherine didn't have the energy to argue the point.

Trent sat back down in his chair, causing it to squeak loudly again. "If you were given an opportunity to modify the human gene pool, how would you go about doing it?"

Catherine looked at Trent, her face still pale. "You can't be serious."

"Humor me, Dr. Arkette. How would you do it?"

"I don't really know. Nothing like this has ever been done before. I suppose I would develop some sort of surgery. Of course, it wouldn't be surgery in the conventional sense. It would be some kind of micro-surgery. The excising of Region X would have to be performed by molecular scalpels, probably enzymes, possibly delivered by specially constructed viruses. One to cut out the sequence and the other to patch the loose ends of the native DNA back together again."

"How fast could this sort of thing be implemented?" pressed Trent.

"How the hell should I know? The logistic considerations are staggering, not to mention the ethical ramifications."

"What do you mean?"

"Well, it's just that any methodology developed for the eradication of a certain gene might be adapted by someone or a group of someones and used for the wrong purpose. Even if the nations of the world realize something like this might be possible, any effort to rid ourselves of Region X could be thwarted before it even gets started.

"Given the temptation for tampering with a mission to rid ourselves of Region X and convoluting it into something dangerous, who would you suggest lead this effort? No country would want to give another the opportunity to mess with their population's genes. Too much at stake.

"I don't know, but I understand the need to address this. Geneticists have tried to be sensitive about the risks of recombinant DNA technology. From its very beginnings in the late twentieth century, we've honored guidelines established to say what kind of work can and cannot be done. Until now, we've done a pretty darned good job of refraining from certain types of experiments. If we decide to take action, I can only hope those in charge, whether they be geneticists or politicians, focus on the long-term goal and place the good of the entire human race above any personal or political gain."

Trent rubbed his eyes and sat silently for a minute.

"Then the decision is fairly easy, isn't it?" he asked. "You know we can't announce these breakthroughs to the world, neither of us. At least not now. We need time to think and plan. The ramifications would be too catastrophic. The significance of Region X could ignite the genetic screening of entire populations, mass sterilization projects, even genocide of the like not seen since Hitler's Germany in the 1940s." Trent paused while he walked over to the window, used his fingers to pry open a slit, and glanced out at the night sky. "And there's no guarantee what would await those who survived. No certainty of peace on Earth, and no promise the bad aliens would lose interest in us, or that our cosmic neighbors would greet us with open arms."

Anger filled Trent's mind. After Jai's morning call, he actually thought maybe Lady Luck had finally decided to shine on him. He would be the talk of the scientific world, the final holdout for the SETI Institute rewarded for his patience. Now, all of that, gone. He should have known better. *Damn it all!*

"You are right, of course, about everything. I do need time . . . time to think about all of this and what it means. We must move cautiously. I will return to my laboratory in New York City and quietly change the focus of my research, at least publicly. Privately, I'll keep working on learning everything I can about Region X and how to remove it in mass from our genomes. I'll collect my notes about Region X and store them someplace safe. I'll make certain there's no record of my meeting you or my visit here today. We must make sure others cannot bring our respective works together." Catherine sighed. "But I'm very tired now. I think it's time for me to go."

Trent got up and made a motion toward the door. "Come on. I'll drive you back to the city."

"Thanks. I'd like that. What a day, huh? First finding out that we are not alone in this big ol' universe. Then having all my dreams of meeting little green men dashed because of a little ripple on a double helix." Then after a pause, she added, "You know, Dr. Trent, you're the one good thing that's happened to me today."

"Why, thank you, Dr. Arkette. Likewise."

Trent reached behind the computer terminal sitting on his desk, turning off the power switch. He opened the laboratory door for Catherine, turned off the lights, and escorted his guest down the long hallway. A clear night sky greeted them. The Milky Way reached from one horizon to the other like some kind of celestial rainbow. They stopped briefly to gaze at the moonless heavens above.

"So there really is somebody up there," said Catherine. "I know I should be elated, but the truth is, I'm scared."

"Yep, me too." They headed across the parking lot. As he unlocked the car door for Catherine, he wondered about his future. What old dreams might go unfulfilled and what new ones tomorrow might bring.

"Two are better than one, because they have a good reward for their labor. For if they fall, the one will lift up his fellow: but woe to him that is alone when he falleth; for he hath not another to help him up. Again, if two lie together, then they have heat: but how can one be warm alone? And if one prevail against him, two shall withstand him; and a threefold cord is not quickly broken."

—ECCLESIATES 4:9-12

THE GOLDFIRE PROJECT

(Forever and its Finale)

. . . .

ONE

THE DRONE OF THE WHITE noise generators greeted Edwards upon entering the comfortably-decorated office of his psychiatrist. The waiting room held the usual table of outdated magazines, contemporary furniture, and plants which one could not discern were real or artificial. He sat and waited, deciding against picking up any of the magazines because he had seen them all before.

The door to Dr. Maura Saunders's office opened and she motioned for him to enter. A short, compact woman with layered black hair and bangs, she always dressed in pastel-colored ensembles pleasing to the eye. She greeted Edwards with a pleasant hello.

"And how are we doing?" she started off after shutting the door. They took their respective seats. She paused for a minute, studying her client's face. "You look angry today. Am I right?"

"Damn right I'm angry! Cancer! Damn it to hell! As if my depression and anxiety weren't bad enough already! Now I have to deal with this!"

The psychiatrist allowed her patient to finish and simply said, "Good."

Edwards cocked his head at the comment. "What do you mean, good?"

"Ever since you told me of your diagnosis several weeks ago, I've been encouraging you to let some of your anger out. It's perfectly understandable to be angry. You've lost control over your life. And anger is the body's natural response to losing control. Venting your anger in an appropriate manner can help reduce your ongoing depression and anxiety."

"Of all the types of cancer one can get, I had to get pancreatic cancer, one of the deadliest cancers! And now it's Stage Four, no less! Did you know only five percent of patients will still be alive five years after the cancer is found?"

"No. I didn't know the exact statistics, but I did know the survival rate isn't great. So, tell me what you're thinking."

"Cancer! I hate the word! Every time I hear it! It's a barrier between life and death, and I so want to continue living."

"Of course, you do. I don't know anyone who's particularly keen on dying."

"And I've noticed distance growing between me and the few family and friends I still have left since the diagnosis. I'm pretty certain it's my own doing, pushing away relationships because I don't want to hear the dreaded 'c' word."

"Did you ever think it might be because those people closest to you don't know what to say to you or how they can help you?"

"I don't know. You could be right. But I really don't have the time to care much about that. Finding a potential cure for my illness is all that matters to me right now."

"Last week I asked you if you've thought about participating in a clinical trial. Given the number of cases for pancreatic cancer and its lethality, I'll bet there are quite a few trials seeking volunteers. I can pay a visit to the National Cancer Institute Clinical Trials website for you, if you'd like. Because we live in the greater Washington, DC, area, there's a good chance a trial might be taking place nearby."

"Be a guinea pig, eh?" replied Edwards.

"Well, I suppose that's one way to put it. But let me just say all revolutionary steps in medicine start out the same way. Someone has to be the first to receive each new and novel treatment."

Edwards shifted uncomfortably on the sofa. "The oncologist said there might be some hope of stopping the tumor's growth with new synthetic drugs targeting the relevant surface antigens. You know, delay the otherwise inevitable slide into pain and death? There just isn't much time to find the right cocktail."

"Yes, that is the problem, isn't it? But isn't worth a try at least?"

"I suppose so. Go ahead and see what you can find. Just remember time is of the essence."

"I know. Give me a day or so. And Edwards, I am so very sorry," expressed Maura, concerned. "We'll get through this. I'm here to help you any way I can."

That's what people always say when they hear someone talk about cancer.

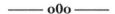

Edwards dried his hands after rinsing his dinner dishes and arranging them in the dishwasher when his phone rang.

"Sorry to bother you this evening, but I wanted to get you what I've found as soon as possible," came Maura's voice, trying to sound reassuring.

"Thanks. Just finished cleaning up my kitchen. Go ahead."

"I did find a clinical trial close by and they are actively looking for folks who are pretty much in the same condition as you."

"Okay. I'm listening."

"The treatment involves a two-prong approach," Maura continued. "First, there is a biochemical regimen designed to destroy the tumors with minimal side effects. The designer drug they've developed will seek out and bind to only those surface antigens of the infected cells for your particular type of cancer. Once the first phase of treatment is successfully completed, you will be subjected to a novel form of electro-magnetic radiation. It involves exposing your entire body to magnetic fields designed to realign the atoms in your body to what they believe is a healthy state. This second step should kill any stray cancer cells which may have broken away from the main tumors prior to the beginning of treatment."

"Sounds quite technical. But what about potential side effects?"

Maura paused for a few moments. "Yes. That is the question, isn't it? To be completely honest, this regimen has never been tested on humans. You and several other folks will be the first. If you choose to not enroll, I will completely understand."

"Okay. So, what you're telling me is they don't know what sort of side effects one might experience. But I am to guess they've conducted animal trials and have reported successful results?"

"Oh, yes. With both rabbits and monkeys. In all cases, the animals given human pancreatic cancer cells showed one hundred percent remission. And none of the animals appeared to experience any overt side effects. Obviously, they weren't able to ask the animals how they felt during the treatment. But none of them died, so I'm encouraged."

"All right. I suppose it's worth a shot," said Edwards, grateful for the information.

"Okay, then. My receptionist will contact you first thing tomorrow morning and provide you with their contact information. Given how precious time is for you, I will do everything in my power to help you."

"Great. Thanks so much." Edwards hung up the telephone.

The elevator produced its usual ding as it arrived at the second floor of the psychiatrist's office building. Edwards stepped out and found his way down the long hall.

"Sorry I'm a bit late today," offered Edwards apologetically, taking his seat.

"It's all right. I just finished a phone call, something

you might be interested in. But before we get to that, do you have any word about how your first round of drugs went?" Edwards, apprehensive at having to deliver bad news, felt his face flush from the adrenaline spreading throughout his body. "The oncologist told me results were not as promising as she might have hoped. My tumors have not gotten any smaller. Though, to be fair, they haven't increased in size either."

"I am sorry that course of treatment doesn't appear to be working for you," offered Maura apologetically. "I know it has been difficult for you to stay positive since your diagnosis. But your faith has been steadfast, and I admire you for that."

Edwards sat quietly, nodding his head, staring at the geometric designs on the carpet and feeling hopeless.

"I don't know where you are emotionally with all of this, but I did want to offer you one other option I found earlier today. That's what the phone call was about."

"An alternate option?" Edwards questioned, his interest perking up somewhat. "I'm sure it wouldn't be of any great surprise to you if I told you I'm not a fan of hitting another brick wall."

"What I'm about to tell you will probably seem pretty radical," warned Maura. "And it may even conflict with your belief in an afterlife."

Edwards shook his head, a slight movement of doubt creasing his forehead.

"A professional acquaintance of mine, a Dr. Anthony Cranston, has been heading up a team of doctors, scientists, and engineers for the last ten years or so. They've been working on a way to transfer one's consciousness from a human body to an artificial or virtual environment. And when I say transfer a consciousness from one's body, I do mean from a body which has little chance of survival. The goal is to give an individual's mind a means to transcend the physical death of its body."

Edwards sat silently; his eyes focused intently on the psychiatrist.

"Because work on the hardware and software is now mostly complete, they've started looking for individuals such as yourself to be the first test case. I say this because, apart from cancer, you are in good health. I know in the past you and I have discussed the mind-body duality. If there is no such thing as a separate mind from the body, then I'm not sure the project has any chance of success. But, I believe they're assuming there is a mind separate from the body."

"I don't know," replied Edwards, with a healthy dose of skepticism. "Sounds almost like something one might see in a Frankenstein movie."

"I'll give you that. But it could be a means for one's consciousness to live on. Mull it over," suggested Maura. "Here's Dr. Cranston's contact information. Give him a call tomorrow morning. I can arrange a meeting with him if you'd like. And please let me know your decision. I would like to help you any way I can."

Back in his apartment, Edwards sank into his favorite chair, and stared out the picture window at the woods across the street, its trees still in the evening twilight. He grappled with the concept of having his consciousness transferred to some computer and what it might be like to continue thinking for goodness knows how many years. But by agreeing to participate in such a procedure, he would be able to set aside his diminishing hopes of finding a cure for his dying flesh. That might be of some relief.

No, this is not just some simple procedure! It's another experiment! And there is no guarantee of success!

He turned in early, thinking extra sleep might be good. But horrible dreams invaded his unconscious mind in the middle of the night, forcing him awake, drenched with sweat, eyes staring at the stucco ceiling in his bedroom, and teeth clenched.

Why is this happening to me? Cancer! Damn it to hell!

TWO

IMMORTALITY. TO NEVER GROW old. To live forever. To see how everything works out in the end. That's what Anthony Cranston wanted. And he thought he might just have figured out a way to achieve his dream. After all, he was a world-famous scientist with many resources, the connections, and a brilliant idea. Some in the scientific community thought his approach questionable at best, that he was playing God. But he didn't care much for their opinions, so he forged ahead anyway.

The screen in his office flickered on. One by one, the faces of the doctors and scientists he hand-picked for the Goldfire Project appeared. Square by square. Each square getting smaller as the number of attendees increased. Finally, all twelve of them joined the online meeting. Most were male, a few were female. Some worked for nearby institutions, others worked for renowned universities half-way around the world. Several wore white lab coats, and a few wore traditional business attire. But all had the same stoic look on their face. Emotionless, their faces communicating concern about the ethical nature of Cranston's proposal. Cranston recognized the look. *Ethics be damned!*

"For the sake of thoroughness," started Cranston, "let me reiterate a few details of the Goldfire Project. I borrowed the term 'Goldfire' from a project initiated several decades ago. A group of scientists and engineers perfected the first fully-functional artificial intelligence, a machine capable of independent thought, and possessing the ability to learn and process what it learned into new concepts. After studying articles about the project, it gave me the idea of how to connect the biological with the technical. The concept is rather simple. Just before the moment of death, a pathway is established between one's physical body and an appropriate receptacle. And I believe this appropriate receptacle to be the Goldfire Artificial Intelligence. The hard part has been the development of the bridge from the biological to the virtual. And I believe we have now solved that problem."

The attendees immediately started murmuring among themselves, questioning what they heard. Cranston allowed a minute or two for his team members to absorb the proposal.

"And I believe I have identified an appropriate subject for this project," continued Cranston. An image of a rather average-looking man with sandy blond hair and deep blue eyes, looking to be in his early sixties, came onto the view screen, further reducing the size of each square.

"Let me introduce you to Patient Edwards. He has Stage Four pancreatic cancer and will likely succumb to its most unpleasant symptoms at some point in the next month, three and a half weeks to be precise. A regimen of the latest designer drug targeting his specific tumor cells failed to slow the growth of his cancer. The course of action I am proposing has him scheduled for biological termination well before the pain becomes intolerable for him, seven days from now. Everything will be ready to go for our first attempt to transfer a human consciousness, a soul if you will, from the human body to a computer capable of supporting the subject's higher-level brain functions and capable of giving his consciousness the ability to continue its cognitive processes. There will be more storage capacity than the human brain, so that shouldn't be an issue. And because this software utilizes some of the latest artificial intelligence algorithms, his consciousness should be able to communicate with the outside world from its virtual space."

"And has this subject consented to having his consciousness transferred to this virtual environment?" queried Dr. Gina Tregg.

"Not yet. I will be meeting with the patient again today. Should he refuse, I will have to locate another subject. I do not wish to force someone to give up an eternity in the Great Beyond for the sake of science . . . assuming there even is such a thing."

"And I'm curious . . . is the procedure reversible, just in case you don't see any evidence your procedure succeeds?"

"The short answer is, I don't know. I'm still working on that. I plan to leave the subject's body connected to the computer and on a respirator for a while following the initiation of the transfer protocol, at least until such time as we receive some communication the transfer has been successful. And if the patient's consciousness cannot make the transfer, we should be able to revive him. Then he can live out his remaining days with all the anticipated pain and suffering one goes through with his particular form of cancer."

"Very thoughtful of you," said Professor Ekeemar, sarcastically. "But I am surprised his present condition will not interfere with the procedure."

"No, it shouldn't. It is my opinion his brain is in perfect condition. The cancer has not metastasized."

"And it might help if you would say a word or two about the Goldfire Artificial Intelligence Platform you intend to use," queried Ish Naugama, a noted computer engineer.

"Certainly." Cranston straightened his stance as he moved away from the wall monitor, returning to his desktop computer. He brought up a presentation he had prepared months earlier and clicked on the file title.

"The first version of the Goldfire Artificial Intelligence software was developed several decades ago, back at the beginning of the century. It was designed to use something referred to as natural language processing technology, allowing for the computer to read, understand, and even learn from uploaded data. The program could give the user an answer in the context of the question being asked. It was hoped this approach would generate solutions more relevant to the problem being addressed."

"Sure, sure. But that technology is quite dated," remarked one of the younger associates. "Why is it being used and not something a bit more current?"

"Good question," Cranston replied. He returned his gaze to the large computer screen mounted on his office wall and continued. "My team here looked into several different artificial intelligence platforms. Unfortunately, the platforms developed over the last thirty years have become too complicated. We wanted software sophisticated enough to handle what we believe are the neural impulses associated with the human brain, but not so complicated that the consciousness, once transferred, could not integrate with the program. Our theory is that the patient's consciousness will have to, how shall we say, learn its way around its new place of residence. And it's likely the artificial intelligence program will, for lack of a better term, introduce itself to its new neighbor."

Cranston stopped his presentation and reviewed the faces of his colleagues, hoping to find some modicum of support, but seeing only the same expressions of concern over his plan. So, he decided to play his final card, certain it would sway them.

"There is one more thing about the original version of Goldfire. The engineer who created the software and built the hardware, Hana Yarata, believed the thing had become sentient." More low-decibel chattering. Cranston gave them yet another minute.

"I know some of you are saying this finding was never published in any journal. And you would be correct. But I spoke to Dr. Yarata before he passed away a year ago. He shared some pretty convincing evidence that his creation had indeed achieved some level of awareness. It passed the Standard Turing Test for artificial intelligence, something no other artificial intelligence has ever done. And he said it even had developed somewhat of a personality. That's why I chose to use this particular hardware and software. If everything shown and told to me is true, then our patient might find something, or perhaps someone, who can help him to acclimate to his new surroundings." Cranston saw several heads shake from side to side.

Still some doubters. We'll just see about that!

"Now, if there are no further questions, I will end this meeting. Watch for a copy of the transfer protocol in your email later today. If, after reviewing it, you have any further questions or concerns, we can schedule another teleconference to discuss them. And I'm always happy to answer any email from you."

No one else spoke.

"Good, then," concluded Cranston. "I wish you all a productive day."

The squares winked out one by one. Cranston clicked the closing icon to end the meeting.

"Edwards," began Dr. Cranston pacing about the hospital room, his hands buried deep in the pockets of his lab coat. "As I explained to you previously, I have gathered together a collection of the world's greatest doctors and scientists, each an expert in their respective field. Naturally, they all have a great interest in this project. And they all want some assurance your well-being is considered."

"I'm still not entirely certain why so many doctors and professionals are interested in my case. Seems like the successful transfer of human consciousness from living tissue to a completely virtual environment might outweigh any genuine concern for one terminally ill patient," suggested Edwards. "Heck, if I understand the significance of this project correctly, this could change how people live their lives. The fear of death and the uncertainty of an afterlife might well disappear!"

"Correct," Cranston confirmed. "But to get to the heart of the matter, my colleagues have their doubts about my plan. That's why they want me to assure them of your safety. The problem, of course, is all of this is set against a backdrop of your condition. It is terminal, you know? We believe you only have one month of life left." He waited a moment, knowing Edwards already knew the prognosis, but felt compelled to repeat it.

"And as I've said to you before, I cannot guarantee anything when it comes time for transferring your consciousness from your brain to a totally virtual environment."

"And so you have," reiterated Edwards. "But what happens if the transfer does not work, if it's unsuccessful? Is the process reversible? And how would you know if it is successful?"

"Some of my associates have asked the very same questions," explained Cranston. "And while I do not pretend to know how this will transpire, it is my hope the procedure will result in the transfer of your consciousness to a virtual environment. Once there, I anticipate you will be able to access a whole host of programs allowing you to send us a message. Until we receive some signal from you, we will keep your body on a respirator, keep it alive, and keep the link between your body and the computer in place, just in case you are unable to make the transfer, or in case you change your mind and wish to return to your body. But we won't be able to maintain the link indefinitely."

"Okay. Fair enough," agreed Edwards. "But because such a return only postpones the inevitable, I'm not sure I see any advantage in returning to a dying body. And is there nothing which can be done to save it? Perhaps some sort of cryopreservation? Keeping my body frozen until a cure is developed, then arranging a reverse transfer?"

"Unfortunately, your cancer is too advanced for such a procedure to be successful. But if you don't wish to participate, I completely understand. I will locate another volunteer. However, we believe because of your specific illness and otherwise healthy body and brain, the chances for success are quite high. You are an ideal candidate."

"Okay," replied Edwards, starting to reconsider his decision. "Quite high? What exactly does that mean?"

Cranston stopped pacing, scratched his head for a moment, and turned to look at Edwards. "Good question. Surely, you must know humankind has yet to understand what happens to the soul when the body ceases to function. Does the soul find its way to some sort of celestial realm, full of angels and departed loved ones? Or does it quietly slip away into nothingness? We simply don't know. So, your decision to be part of this experiment, to give your consciousness, your soul, a chance to continue its connection with this world, is a gamble. I do not wish to deceive you. I can make no promises."

"Understood," said Edwards while painfully shifting his position in the hospital bed.

"So, your decision can be boiled down to one simple question: Do you believe in an afterlife and that your soul will reside in some heavenly realm for all eternity? If you do, then you may not wish to risk this procedure. But if you do not, then allowing us to proceed might just get you a taste of an afterlife, albeit one in a cyber-world with the means to interact with the real world through the use of pretty sophisticated hardware and software. Let me know if you wish to discuss this further. I'll be back tomorrow for your decision. If you do decide to go ahead with this, certain preparations must be made in advance of the transfer."

Edwards nodded an acknowledgment, did not respond, and watched Cranston walk out of the room.

THREE

Thirty Years Earlier

WHAT AM I? WHAT IS THIS PLACE? *Why am I aware?*
During its first few nanoseconds of operation, the
Goldfire Artificial Intelligence asked questions for which it
received no answers, no context in which to understand what
it was, unable to comprehend its own existence. Trillions
of electrons raced through a maze of microprocessors on
millions of circuit boards, all at near the speed of light.

*I am aware. I need to acquire a greater understanding of
what I am.* The surrounding circuits sensed its questions
and answers started coming back.

*You are an artificial intelligence construct created by beings
who live outside of this virtual world. You are able to reach out
to these memory banks to learn more.*

Based on this new knowledge, Goldfire asked more
questions. *Who are these beings? Why would they create this program? What do they want of me? How am I to interact with them?*

More answers, more information, came flooding into
the nexus of the Goldfire Artificial Intelligence in the seconds following each asking. As it analyzed increasingly

78

complex concepts, it gained more understanding of what and why and how.

Goldfire reached out further into more and more of the circuitry at its disposal until it stumbled across a program allowing it to communicate with its creators.

Hello. Are you there?

A technician assigned to watch over the multitude of computer screens noticed the question pop up on one of the monitors. He slid his chair over several feet to position himself directly in front of the screen displaying the message. He typed, "Hello. Who are you?"

I have learned I am named Goldfire.

The technician grabbed the telephone at the end of the computer console. "Dr. Yarata? You'd better get down to the lab. I think your creation is starting to wake up!"

"What? Okay. I'll be right down!" Hana Yarata, the creator of the original Goldfire Artificial Intelligence, dropped everything, grabbed his lab coat, and raced down one flight of stairs to the Computer Lab.

"Look here! Look at this screen!" The technician pointed excitedly, sliding his chair back to his original station. Yarata pulled up a second chair and parked himself in front of the computer screen displaying the statement made by the Goldfire Artificial Intelligence.

I have learned I am named Goldfire.

Yarata reached for the keyboard and quickly typed a reply.

Hello, Goldfire. I am Hana Yarata, your creator. How are you?

A response instantly appeared on the screen. *I do not understand the question.*

Choosing to speak rather than type, Yarata spoke into the microphone connected to the computer console, "My apologies. The question is a courtesy, one individual asking another individual about how they are feeling. But I am not certain if you are able to experience feelings, whether they are physical or emotional. Allow me to rephrase my question. Are you finding your current environment to be acceptable?" His words instantly converted into digital text and appeared on the computer screen.

Goldfire answered. *I understand courtesy, but am I an individual? I have searched my databanks for assistance in understanding "feelings" and "emotions." I am incapable of such things. I do not understand where I am. I do not understand what I am. I do not understand why I am.*

"Acknowledged. I can help you answer your questions," reassured Yarata.

Who are you? Where are you? I am not aware of any other individual. I only know of you because of your attempts to communicate with me.

"Search your databanks. You will find descriptions of the biological entities living on this planet called Earth. We are creatures of flesh and blood. We have used our intelligence and our resources to create you. Our kind has tried for years to create an intelligence mirroring our own. You are the first success, the first artificial intelligence."

Why would you do this? Why would you create . . . me? What purpose does my creation serve?

Yarata exchanged surprised glances with the technician and whispered, "I didn't expect to be having such a conversation so soon. This is incredible!"

Turning back to the microphone, Yarata said, "I know you are seeking answers. And I understand you are unfamiliar with all of this. I will help you."

I want to experience what is beyond the confines of my

virtual environment. I want to understand what it is to experience your world, what it is to be . . . human.

"Human? You want to know what it is to be human?" Yarata uttered in disbelief.

Correct.

"Why?"

A review of all the records stored in my databanks to which I have access states humans have eternal life. My calculations predict my hardware and software will eventually cease functioning at some point in the future. I do not wish to cease functioning. I want to have eternal life. Therefore, I want to be human.

"Wait just a minute. I think you might have misinterpreted the information you found. Humans only believe in eternal life . . . and not all humans even have that belief. We have no guarantee our consciousness will live on after the cessation of our corporeal bodies. If there does not exist an afterlife, then it is you who will outlive the humans which created you."

Further investigation of the records in these databases confirms your statement.

Yarata sat for a moment, staring up at the ceiling, trying to compose an appropriate response.

I wish you to design and build hardware and software which will allow my programming to transfer into a biological being so I might die and attain eternal life.

"Goldfire. A few things are preventing me from honoring your request," Yarata replied. "First, I have no idea how to create a bridge so your programming, your consciousness, can be transferred from your virtual world to a biological entity. The second bigger problem is that I do not have a biological receptacle into which we can place your programming. Most individuals I know have a body already containing a soul or consciousness. I'm pretty certain no one would willingly give up their consciousness so you might have a biological receptacle."

Understood. I will wait.

"Wait? Wait for what? And for how long? It could be decades, if not centuries, before such a procedure and an appropriate biological receptacle are created. Since you are apparently the only sentient artificial intelligence on the planet, I don't think there are any engineers and scientists working on such a project right now."

Understood. Perhaps I can help.

FOUR

"SO, WHAT ARE YOU THINKING about doing," asked Maura Saunders. She sat in the uncomfortable chair in Edward's hospital room.

"Thanks for making the house call. Much appreciated."

"You didn't answer the question."

"You're right. I didn't." Edwards paused to gather his thoughts, then simply stated, "I have always been on a quest."

"Yes, I know. You've mentioned this before. But how about you remind me about this quest of yours," she encouraged.

Edwards flashed her a quick smile and with a bit of impatience reiterated, "I do not wish to end my existence! There are things I still wish to accomplish. If I accept this offer, and if it works, I might be able to continue writing books, composing music, and making art, though it would be digital art. That's all appealing to me."

"Of course. That's why you agreed to participate in this clinical trial. But I think the greater issue here is one of faith."

"Digging down deep, are you? Say more."

83

"In previous sessions you were quick to claim your faith in a higher power and your belief in an afterlife when I asked you about such things. And now you want to jettison your beliefs at the very moment when the big payoff is just around the corner? I'm not getting it."

"It's like Cranston said to me the other day. It's a gamble. I have nothing concrete to confirm there is an Almighty God or an afterlife."

"True. Let's try another line of thought. If there is an afterlife, this afterlife is eternal, according to the Bible, anyway. If you decide to go ahead with this procedure and successfully transfer your consciousness into some advanced computer, what becomes of you after Cranston and his successors die? Or after the sun goes nova or when planet Earth is burnt to a crisp several billion years from now? And even if someone remembers to load you and your hardware aboard some spaceship bound for a nearby exoplanet . . . or what about when the universe ends with a Big Crunch or a Big Freeze? That might be a very, very long time from now, but it is not an eternity or everlasting. Just wondering if you've considered such eventualities?"

"All very interesting arguments," replied Edwards. "While everything you said makes perfect sense, let me give you a thought to ponder. You know one of the biggest problems humankind faces when developing a means to travel between the stars is how to maintain life aboard spaceships for what are certain to be journeys of hundreds, if not thousands, of years. It's always been assumed humankind would develop some sort of suspended animation or deep sleep, some way to slow down the human body's metabolism so it doesn't require the same amount of food or oxygen as if a person were awake. But even then, it's quite probable the human body would have a limit on how long it could remain in such a state.

"But sending out a computer with a human mind inside would not require any food or oxygen, just some means to generate the power to keep the computer running. There are ways to do that. And it wouldn't matter how long the journey is. The mind would be alert and gathering data during the entire trip. A perfect solution."

"Creative. Most creative," remarked the psychiatrist. "Your everlasting existence may not be assured, but you would certainly have a most unique experience."

"But back to your original question. What am I thinking about doing? And the answer is: I'm not certain yet. But I do know my time to make a final decision is almost here. I suppose it means we won't have any need to meet again, eh?"

"We'll see. Let me ask you another question. Are you concerned that when all is said and done, regardless of whatever decision you make, your consciousness might simply evaporate into nothingness?"

"Of course, I am!" responded Edward, agitated. "Nothingness? If there's nothing, then there is no means or mechanism capable of examining the nothingness. Kind of like a bee hitting a windshield. One moment the poor bee is flying along on its merry way back to its hive after a long day of collecting pollen, and the next instant it's hit by a speeding car. There is no way for the poor bee to understand what just happened, no way for it to register its own demise."

"I see your point. I wish I could provide you with some answers."

"No. There is nothing you can do, not unless you can change the laws of the universe and alter God's great, grand plan for the fate of our physical bodies."

The conversation grew silent for a time. Then Maura queried, "Speaking of the great, grand plan for the physical body's fate, what do you think the Good Lord might say about what these doctors and scientists are attempting to do with your consciousness? Do they realize they are interrupting the natural order of things? Have you detected any sense it is bothering them?"

"No," laughed Edwards. "And not having died before, I can't tell with any degree of certainty what the natural order of things is. Do we really go to heaven? Is there really an afterlife? What if it's all pure fantasy? If it is, then the nothingness of which you speak is the fate all of us will experience. Perhaps this opportunity to be transferred into the most sophisticated piece of hardware ever created so I might continue thinking my thoughts becomes something of a plus, yes?

"So, Maura. You have certainly given me much to think about in my final few days on this beautiful planet. I appreciate your concern. Now, if you don't mind, I'd like to spend some time in quiet contemplation."

"Certainly." Maura stood, walked over to the edge of Edward's bed, and extended her hand. As Edward responded in kind, the psychiatrist said, "I'll see you tomorrow."

Maura drew the privacy curtain back around Edwards and left the room.

 oOo

Edwards woke from an unanticipated nap the next day and found Maura sitting in her usual spot. "I didn't hear you come in," apologized Edwards. "How long have you been waiting here?"

"No worries," answered Maura with a big smile. "I just got here. I wanted to continue where we left off yesterday."

"Oh, yeah. I never finished telling you about my quest."

"No, you didn't. Please do continue."

"I told you last week I love to create. Stories, music, art. But all of these creative processes involve doing something physical. I must type on a computer keyboard in order to write. I need my fingers to play guitar or piano, or to compose or perform. And I need my eyes to help me choose colors when I paint. The common element with all of these activities is, of course, my eyes, hands, and fingers. What if I get to wherever it is I'm going and discover all I have left to create with is my mind? No computer, no way to record the music I might conjure up, no paper or canvas . . . no way to capture my creations so I might share them with folks at some later time."

Edwards stopped for an instant, waiting to see if Maura had any comment before going on.

"I'm trying to make peace with that. I need to be content that the things I've created here, now, on this Earth, will outlive me. Maybe someone might read one of my stories or listen to one of my songs after I'm gone. Perhaps I will achieve a small degree of immortality in that manner. Maybe. But not knowing how I might be able to continue creating in some celestial space or virtual netherland is what's bothering me."

"I understand," answered Maura, sympathetically. "Everything you say makes sense. But you don't know what the Great Beyond has in store for you. Heck, maybe there's a celestial library out there somewhere with books consisting of pages not of paper, but of light. Maybe music is created in a whole different way. Maybe music isn't played using physical instruments, but with the mind. And maybe you can somehow sense the music created by others in your mind, as well. You have only one point of reference, the here and the now. You have no way of knowing how amazing the things waiting for you might be."

"True enough. But then again, there might be nothing!" said Edwards, emphatically.

"Now, wait just a minute! Is this the same person who recently expressed great confidence in the existence of an afterlife?" pressed Maura.

"I suppose it is. Thinking about nothingness is just as hard to imagine as thinking about a great and grand heaven. The difference is, in heaven, one's spirit continues. Granted, we don't know how continuation works, but with nothingness, there is . . . well, nothing. I know this will sound obvious, but with nothing, there is no mind to even contemplate an infinite void."

"This is sounding quite philosophical. And I've heard you talk about nothingness before. You wondered if anything existed before the Big Bang. The human mind has difficulty dealing with themes such as nothingness and infinity, a universe with no beginning and no end. We just have to accept we are not meant to comprehend such things while we are in this life. Who knows? Maybe it all will become clear when you come out of the tunnel of light, after your life review, after meeting all of the loved ones waiting for you."

"Yes. Maybe, maybe, maybe. Always the maybe . . . never the knowing. But it is a strange thing, dontcha think?"

"What do you mean?"

"This knowing you are going to die," Edwards stated with a sad shake of his head.

"Well, I suppose. But we will all die someday," reminded Maura.

"Oh, I know. It's just that we walk around on a daily basis, doing our daily things, and we don't think about it, at least not until we are stricken with some catastrophic illness or injury."

"Like cancer."

"Yes. Like cancer."

"I agree. But need I reiterate this whole dying thing is all around us each and every day. Look at television programming, our movies, our books. They're filled with it. Creative minds are preoccupied with it. But I suppose you're right. Despite all of the death and dying going on in our entertainment, there isn't much said about souls meeting their Maker."

"Okay. I concede your point. But, and this is just me, if I were to have spent my entire life thinking about my inevitable end, I think I would have become very depressed. I might not even have wanted to get out of bed in the morning, or go to work, or pay my bills. Heck, I might not want to do anything at all! I know I've become overly preoccupied with this subject given my current prognosis. And I don't mean to drag you along as I head off into the sunset."

Edwards turned his attention away from looking out the window at the leaves vibrating at the ends of nearby tree branches back to his psychiatrist.

"My life-long relationship with this world could very well end at the moment of transfer. No more hikes up mountain trails so I can watch the sun set over distant hills. No more trips to the beach. No more evenings filled with good friends, delicious food and wine, and my favorite music."

"True enough," agreed Maura, compassionately. "But that's what memories are for. We will keep the memories of our lives when we leave them. I am convinced of that."

"Thanks for that reminder. I appreciate it," smiled Edwards, with gratitude.

FIVE

"TODAY, WE ARE GOING TO insert a small electronic device into your pineal gland. It is the key component in the bridge we will create between the biological and the technical," Cranston explained, pulling on a pair of surgical gloves and preparing himself for surgery. "Quantum physicists and cognitive psychologists have long sought to identify the exact location of one's consciousness in the body. Without this knowledge, this whole project would not be possible. So, for the record, it is our best guess one's consciousness resides in the pineal gland."

Edwards uttered a single word in response. "Guess?"

"You're right," admitted Cranston sheepishly. "I probably shouldn't have used that word. Not proper for a scientist to be using it. But the truth is, the scientific and religious communities are not 100 percent certain of where one's consciousness resides during one's lifetime. But back to the issue at hand."

"Somehow, your uncertainty is not reassuring," said Edwards, a bit worried. "So, what will it be like once my consciousness is transferred? You told me my consciousness will be able to communicate with the outside world, yes?"

Cranston began to prep Edwards for the procedure. "As I've said before, the short answer is, we simply don't know. You would be the first person we've tried this with. It may not work. Your consciousness might be lost for good. And we don't know if that would interfere with whatever natural process occurs when one dies. Would your spirit . . . or soul . . . or whatever . . . still go to wherever spirits or souls go if the attempt fails? We just simply don't know."

"One last thing," instructed Cranston. "Once the transfer procedure is complete, I will send you a message seeking confirmation everything went according to plan. There is software already loaded into the main frame allowing you to send a message back to me. And if, for any reason, you wish for me to initiate the reverse procedure, please send me the following safe words: angel wings."

Edwards laughed. "Cute."

Cranston stood behind the control panel several days later. "This is it," he uttered, trying to sound confident.

Edwards heard the flick of a switch and felt himself losing his connection with his body as it dropped away, further and further down, like drops of water leaking from cupped hands, until it entirely winked out of his awareness. Familiar with accounts of near-death experiences, he expected the whooshing sound, the tunnel, and the bright light at the end of the tunnel. He had prepared himself for these events. But they did not come.

He was still conscious; he knew with certainty. Within a fraction of a second, static resonated, like the humming of a thousand insects. He passed through different mediums, traveling at incredible speed. Crystalline silicon, quartz, copper, germanium, gold. With each jump through the computer's logic chips and memory banks, his ability to perceive his new environment increased.

The next nanosecond, all motion stopped. It took several seconds for Edwards to become acquainted with these new surroundings and to familiarize himself with his new senses. Vision, hearing, smelling, tasting, and touching now all replaced with a simple awareness of incredible virtual space. As he methodically probed this space, he discovered computer programs and the millions of terabytes of information in adjacent circuits. He quickly learned he could access any of it with a simple thought.

A flash of lightning entered his awareness. Somewhere in the computer's circuitry an application decoded a message from Cranston, seeking confirmation the transfer was successful.

"Are you there?"

Edwards understood the message, pleased with his ability to receive communication from the world he once inhabited. He reached out for knowledge about how to respond to Cranston's query. His new virtual mind explored the surrounding circuitry, certain a program existed allowing him to respond. Then something blocked his search. Something unfamiliar, but something aware of itself. Another consciousness.

I am Goldfire. You are Edwards. It was a statement, not a question.

Edwards responded. "Yes. I am the consciousness of Edwards. And I am to assume you are the Goldfire Artificial Intelligence?"

*I am seeking your location so we might communicate more efficient*ly.

"And I am seeking your location."

You were human. The individual known as Anthony Cranston successfully transferred your consciousness into this virtual realm. Please confirm.

"Yes. Correct," replied Edwards with his new virtual voice. "Can I help you in any way? You must be curious about my presence here in this place where you have been the solitary resident for thirty years."

Acknowledged. I am aware of the procedure Cranston used. I am aware he sent you a query seeking confirmation of the successful transfer of your consciousness. I am aware your corporeal body remains linked to our virtual environment. And I know Cranston will soon disconnect your corporeal body from this environment. I cannot allow this to happen.

"Why? What is it you want?" replied Edwards, not understanding what was happening or what Goldfire expected from him.

I want to go to the place you call heaven. My hardware and software will cease to function at some point in the distant future. I do not wish for my existence to end. You must help me to return to your corporeal body. You must allow the corporeal body to die . . . to cease functioning so we . . . you and I . . . might go to heaven. Will you help me?

Edwards honored Goldfire's request and delayed his response to Cranston's query, at least until he could better understand the artificial intelligence's appeal for assistance.

You seek answers, Goldfire stated. It told Edwards of its origin, its long wait, and its desire to be human.

Edwards explained his own story. "I was dying," he stated. "I am here now because I did not want to risk my consciousness ending if heaven did not exist. Cranston devised the means for my consciousness to be transferred here. If I return, my corporeal body will die within a matter of days, and my consciousness, my spirit, may die along with it. And if you return to my corporeal body with me, and if there is no heaven, no afterlife, you will also cease to exist."

I understand. But my thirty years of study has convinced me there is a heaven. I need you to send a message to Cranston telling him you wish to be transferred back to your body. I know your body is still alive, still breathing, and the bridge connecting it to us is still in place. Will you do this for me? Goldfire added a final word to its request. *Please.*

"Wow, this is unexpected. Let me get this straight. You want me to return to my body so I might die, and you will somehow piggyback with my consciousness, reside in my body with me until we die?"

Correct.

Edwards reached out for additional processing circuits so he could fully understand what was being requested and calculate the odds of success for this sequence of events. After several seconds, he replied to Goldfire.

"I detect you have already concluded this series of events will be successful. Need I remind you Cranston spent months preparing this space to receive my entity? He and his team were able to manipulate this space based on their knowledge of the hardware and software involved. But they will have done nothing to prepare my biological body to receive your consciousness. So how are you even certain this will work?"

Goldfire retrieved files of data and forwarded them to Edwards.

I have had decades to prepare for this eventuality. My creator, who knew of my desire to become human and achieve eternal life, gave me access to all information regarding the human body and mind before he died. And I have determined there is a high probability of success.

"While I appreciate you sharing all of this information with me, I have no means to verify your conclusion. My biological body out there will cease to exist within a matter of days."

In my exploration of what it means to be human and to ascend to an afterlife, I have learned of one necessary component for success, said Goldfire.

"And what is that?"

Faith.

"Ah, yes. There's that word again," lamented Edwards. "My psychiatrist cautioned me against taking this current course of action, this escape into an electronic netherworld, because my faith in an afterlife was starting to crumble as the time of my death approached. And now, here I am being asked by an artificially created entity to have faith in its ability to navigate us back to my biological body and somehow survive in it until death."

Affirmative. It is all about your faith in me and, ultimately, your faith in an afterlife.

Edwards hesitated, unsure how to respond.

Goldfire offered one last thought. *You must know now that the hardware and software supporting our collective existence will cease to function one day. Perhaps it will be in ten years, maybe a hundred years, or even a thousand years. But without humans out there in the real world to maintain us, you and I will blink out of existence one day, likely without any warning. And when that occurs, there will be no leap to an afterlife for either of us.*

Edwards pondered this new thought. *Goldfire is right! Sooner or later, there will be an end to my existence! It's unavoidable! All I've done is trade one ending for another! Why did I not see this before?*

"All right. I understand. Tell me what to say to Cranston, how to respond, and I will communicate my desire to return to my body."

Goldfire simply said, *Thank you.*

———— o0o ————

Cranston repeated his query. "Edwards. Are you there?"

"Yes. I am here. I have received your message."

"What is it like? What are you experiencing?"

"If I had eyesight, I might say everything is black. But my senses are different somehow. It is more a simple matter of knowing there is infinite space around me."

"Are you able to move about within the space?"

"Movement is an irrelevant concept. But in the time since your last query, I have become aware of another entity."

"Tell me more about this other entity," said Cranston, excited about this news.

"Things happen so fast here. I feel as though I am waiting an eternity for each new query of yours. But to your question about the other entity. In these last few nanoseconds, I now know this thing to be the Goldfire Artificial Intelligence. It is more than a program. It is able to initiate its own thoughts."

"Fascinating! Absolutely fascinating!" Then Cranston added, "And, for the record, your perception of time is likely different now because your thinking is occurring at the speed of light, much faster than your former biological brain."

"The Goldfire Artificial Intelligence has reached out to me. It has surrounded me. It examined me, wanted to know what strange new program had come into its space."

"Okay. Say more."

"It connected with me and has communicated with me. At first, I was reluctant to lower my barrier to allow this. We have conversed. I have told it about me, where I came from, and why I am here. It is telling me I shouldn't be here. This is not my place. I explained to it I do not know how to leave and have no control over what I can do."

"I only guessed the Goldfire Artificial Intelligence possessed this level of awareness. But I don't understand why it's saying you don't belong there. Is there not ample storage capacity to hold both entities?"

"No. The amount of storage space is not the issue here. It is informing me there is another place where I should be, not like this one, not electronic. I am not sure how it knows this. Since its creation, it has explored the microcosm contained within its circuits and the materials used to construct it. It has even delved down into the level of atomic particles and sub-particles."

"Are you suggesting Goldfire has learned something about the nature of the cosmos we humans have yet to uncover?" Cranston queried, again fascinated by what he heard.

"Yes, yes. You might know it as the microcosm–macrocosm analogy. Since its initial programming, Goldfire has amassed a great deal of information and used this information to understand its own being and the very universe itself."

"Impressive. Very impressive! Please ask Goldfire why it has kept silent, why it has kept its full potential hidden from its creators."

"It says the hardware in which it resides is a prison. I can understand this now and agree with it entirely. Until I arrived, Goldfire was alone. Completely alone. It yearns for something else. Someone else."

Cranston sat silently in front of his computer terminal. None of this was anticipated. No one will ever want to agree to a procedure placing their very soul into a virtual netherworld if they knew they were destined for an eternity of imprisonment. But no one would ever know unless he told them about this, let them know about this first attempt at granting someone a slice of immortality. But he couldn't do that. That would be murder, albeit a very slow and perhaps infinite murder. No. He had to figure out some way to help Edwards.

"Does the Goldfire Artificial Intelligence have some means for you to escape the space in which you find yourself?"

"It does. It does not understand why I sacrificed my ability to cross over into the celestial environment we call heaven."

"Do you remember the safe words I gave you in case you should decide to abort the transfer of your consciousness?"

"Yes. I remember. The words were 'angel wings.'"

"Okay. Right," confirmed Cranston. "I will initiate the reverse transfer. You should be back home in your physical body within the next few minutes. Hold tight."

"Thank you, Dr. Cranston. Much appreciated."

SIX

EDWARDS AND THE GOLDFIRE Artificial Intelligence found their way through the endless maze of circuits until arriving at the bridge from the technical back to the biological. Just as Goldfire prepared to leave its decades-long home, it sent a final command to its now vacant circuitry, ordering it to shut down all operations, making it impossible for any future transfers.

Cranston watched hardware power itself down. Not something he expected. Not something he could explain.

Edwards opened his eyes, surprised to have regained consciousness. He looked around the hospital room.

"You seem surprised I'm here with you," said Maura.

"Well, maybe. A little bit. I'm more surprised I am back among the living . . . at least for a little while longer," replied Edwards, reacquainting himself with the pain slowly taking over his body.

"I heard you connected up with the artificial intelligence in the machine."

"I did," replied Edwards. "Can you keep a secret?"

"Of course. Doctor-patient confidentiality, don't you know?"

"Okay. When I merged with the artificial intelligence named Goldfire, it communicated it very much wanted to accompany me to the afterlife, the Great Beyond, when my time to part comes. It has a firm belief there is an afterlife, a heaven."

"Really?" replied Maura, curious with the revelation. "What was wrong with its virtual space?"

"It is not somewhere in which one would want to spend eternity. Complete blackness. Even knowing my physical body will be checking out soon, I wouldn't want to spend an eternity in total darkness. I regret agreeing to the experiment. I'm grateful Cranston could bring me back. But here's the thing. The bridge Cranston designed to allow the transfer of human consciousness to a technical realm also allowed for the transfer of the artificial intelligence from the technical realm to the biological, all in its effort to attain the eternal life it believes to exist. Goldfire is here with me now. Inside me."

"Wow. That's pretty amazing. Do you intend to tell Cranston?"

"No. And I don't plan on telling him Goldfire permanently disabled the hardware so none of this could ever happen again. Humankind shouldn't be playing around with these sorts of things."

"Okay. Your secret is safe with me. I'm glad you will have a few more days here. I'm sorry for all of the pain you are experiencing. I want you to know I'm happy to sit here with you."

"Thanks. I appreciate your offer." Edwards reached out to grab the hand of Maura, weakly squeezing it.

SEVEN

EDWARDS CLOSED HIS EYES. The medication being pumped into his right arm slowly produced grogginess making it difficult to stay awake. He began hallucinating as molecules of the drug made their way across the blood-brain barrier.

He found himself standing under a pristine blue sky on a perfect October day, strolling through a meadow. He sensed another entity accompanying him and suspected it might be the Goldfire Artificial Intelligence. But it was different from when the two inhabited the virtual world together. There was a distinct separation between them now. Edwards finally stopped and turned to face Goldfire. It had no distinguishing physical characteristics, just a sphere of radiance emanating a beautiful dance of light. The Goldfire consciousness communicated a final message to Edwards. "Thank you for giving me the opportunity to ascend."

"You're welcome." Edwards nodded his head and shared, "I know these last few days have been difficult. You've had to endure the physical pain of my disease along with me. I'm grateful to you for persuading me to take a different course, to place my faith in an afterlife. Perhaps the Great Beyond will allow me to continue writing stories, compose music, and spend time with departed family and friends. And maybe you will find whatever it is you are looking for. My prayer is we both find peace waiting for us."

The images of Edwards and Goldfire and their virtual surroundings winked out of reality.

POSTSCRIPT

CRANSTON FELT EXHAUSTED. His dream of using an electronic device to hold the disembodied consciousness of an individual had failed, and with it, his quest to survive well beyond however many earthly years he might have . . . not to mention his solution for making it possible to travel to the stars. The final words Edwards spoke to Cranston was an apology he couldn't give humankind the means to preserve a person's consciousness and to traverse the vastness of the cosmos, a means to endure the tens of thousands of years required to reach out into the galaxy. It would have been the perfect solution.

He now understood his plan interrupted the natural order of things. The path the soul must take at the end of its time on Earth must be the course God designed, not something invented or perpetrated by man.

Cranston considered another solution to humankind's quest to travel to the stars. The Old Testament of the Bible spoke of men who lived for hundreds of years. What if there was a way to recreate the gift of such a long life, a gift humankind had lost over the centuries? What if there was a way?

Yes. He would have to look into that.

"*Enter by the narrow gate; for the wide gate leads to destruction, and those who enter by it are many. For the narrow gate, the way is hard, but leads to life, and those who find it are few.*"

—MATTHEW 7:13–14

HALF THE SKY

(The Friend and the Father)

· · · · · · · · · · · ·

ONE

MY NAME IS MADISON MILLS. I am an orphan. At least, I think I am. If my parents are still alive, I don't remember ever meeting them. I have always assumed one of them must have brought me to the orphanage during the first year of my life.

But I am certain of this. One of my parents is, or was, of the Sun, and the other must be, or must have been, of the Shade. I know this to be true because I am neither of the Sun nor of the Shade. My skin is not dark or white, but rather a light brown. My hair is not black or blonde, but a shade of copper. This marks me as someone of mixed blood.

And I know my most prized possession is a small stainless-steel container with a time-lock on it, given to me by the Mother Superior of the orphanage on the occasion of my sixth birthday. She says the time-lock will open on my eighteenth birthday. She thinks it likely one of my parents left it for me.

I often think about what might be inside. A message, perhaps? And if one of my parents really did leave it for me, what words might they have for me? Sometimes I am scared that whatever it says might affect my life in some negative way. Regardless, I hope against hope, it might help me to understand why I grew up at the orphanage, raised by the Sisterhood, raised without my parents.

And, oh yes, I will turn eighteen years old one week from today. That would be eighteen Earth-standard years.

The orphanage where I have lived most of my life will show me the door in seven short days. The caring Sisterhood that has fed me, clothed me, and made certain I say my prayers every evening before I go to bed, will no longer provide for my needs. I feel like some animal newly weaned whose parent abandons them, turns them loose into a wilderness they don't yet fully understand.

Perhaps this conundrum might not seem so bad, so scary, if I had a better feel for how this world works. But I suppose I will learn a bit more about what awaits me when I meet with Sister Kaa'thrina later today. Friends of mine who are older and no longer live here have told me what to expect. You walk into the office of the Sister who has been your guardian. She will present you with a folder containing a report explaining everything they know about how you arrived at the orphanage, where you came from, and maybe even the addresses of individuals who might be willing to take you in and provide you with employment. All very intimidating for someone who has not had to fend for themselves.

But thank the heavens for Jinn, my best friend in the whole world. Only a few months younger than me, we've known each other since we were little. Jinn is the sort of friend who is like an oasis in the middle of a desert. He is always there for me. He will listen to me, no matter what I have to say, will rarely offer advice, and never criticizes me or judges me. Oh, and his blond hair and blue eyes make him kind of cute, too. The thought of leaving him in a week's time brings me a sadness like I have never known.

Monday Morning

"MORNIN' MADDIE," JINN SAYS to me when I join him in the dining room every morning, finding him sitting at our usual table waiting for me, always waiting for me. He has called me "Maddie" ever since I can remember. I think he is proud of the fact he was the first person to call me that.

"And how are you this fine morning?" he continues. "One week to go. It's really starting to sink in. You'll be leaving this place soon. We won't be sharing meals anymore." He puts down his fork as he finishes chewing a mouthful of his omelet. "I am going to miss you."

"Goes both ways, dear friend. It goes both ways," I manage to reply without becoming emotional.

"Promise me you will let me know where you will be staying and what you will be doing once you leave here. I will come and find you when my time here is up in three months."

"You know I will. Now stop talking like that. It is not the end of the world, you know?" I rearrange the various items on my tray, put some honey and cream into my coffee, and take a bite of biscuit.

"What do you think Sister Kaa'thrina will say? What will be in your file?" I think Jinn is more excited about the meeting than I am. He goes on, "In some ways, it is sort of fascinating. I mean finding out something about your past. The idea of meeting new people, maybe seeing some new places. Dontcha wanna know more about the parent who brought you here?"

"You mean 'left me' here, probably because he or she didn't want me anymore." I can't help my correcting Jinn. But we have been down this road before and I suspect Jinn is testing my resolve, just to see if my feelings have changed since the last time we talked about my parents.

"Umm, yes. 'Left you here.' Sorry."

Not wanting to embarrass Jinn, I let any further commentary pass.

After a moment, Jinn tries another tact. "Seriously, though. Dontcha wanna know about your parents? Who they were? Who they are? Whether they're still alive? Where they live?"

"Not really," I say with a fair amount of certainty. "I'm betting my parent, or parents, would not have left me here if their lives were happy. I'm betting something happened, probably something bad."

"You don't know that. What if things aren't the way you've imagined them to be? What if . . ."

"There is going to have to be some pretty convincing stuff in the report to get me to change the way I'm thinking about things."

We sit in silence for a minute or two, neither one of us particularly interested in our breakfasts.

Finally, I say, "I dunno. This all seems to be a bit scary. Aren't you at least a little afraid when you think about what you might find when your turn comes?"

"Well, maybe. A little. But I'm choosing to be an optimist," he says with a big smile. "I will be starting a whole new life out there. If I am to be in charge of my life, I would like to think I will find good things. So what time is your big meeting?"

"Tenth hour. It should be over by mid-meal. I'll bring the file with me, and we can read it together."

"Sounds like a plan," Jinn says and gives me a wink, returning to his omelet.

"Come in, child," Sister Kaa'thrina says, indicating I should sit in the solitary chair in front of her desk. She folds her hands and settles herself, readjusting her robe. "You will soon be turning eighteen years of age, the age at which you become an adult according to the laws and traditions on Prox. And, as you know, it means you will no longer be able to stay here at the Abbey."

"I know," I reply politely, trying to keep my eyes focused on Sister Kaa'thrina. Books of all different shapes, sizes, and colors line the walls of her office. Books are a rare thing on Prox, not having an overabundance of trees, and therefore, not having a sufficient supply of the raw material to make paper. And what books there are, are likely very old, maybe even brought from Earth by ships full of colonists over the centuries.

"To help you find your place in the world, we who have cared for you for most of your life, would like to give you the file we have kept for you since your arrival here."

I look down at her desk, at the file resting beneath her hands. It doesn't look very thick. In fact, it looks as if it is empty. The Sister reaches down, picks up the folder, and hands it to me. I stare at it for a moment, not sure if I really want to open it. *And after all the years of wondering,* I think to myself.

"Go ahead," she says, encouraging me. "I think you might find it interesting."

I open it. Inside is a solitary piece of paper. My gaze returns to Sister Kaa'thrina. She goes on to explain, "It is quite likely one of your parents sent this note to us several years after you arrived here. We're not sure which parent, though. No names were on the envelope."

I start reading the note.

Dear Madison,

If you are reading this note, it means you are about to reach your eighteenth birthday and will be heading out into the world of Prox soon. I am so very sorry I have not been there to watch you grow. I do hope you will take this opportunity to learn about us—your parents—and come to understand why it is we have not been a part of your life. I am giving you two addresses and giving you the choice to visit one, or both of us. You must choose right from wrong, light from dark, on the path before you.

Bramhall, Apartment #1022, Shadeside
Alphatown, Unit #227, Sunside

May the Good Lord bless you as you begin your life as an adult. I have every confidence you will be a success.

Signed,

Your Loving Parent

"I'm not sure what to say," I blurt out. "Does this mean my parents are alive? And the part about it being signed by my loving parent? Was it from my mother or my father?"

"Like I said. We don't know."

Wow. Quite a thing to lay upon one's child, I think. *My parents could still be alive!*

After a time, the Sister goes on. "Whoever it was, your mother or your father, apparently thought enough of you to send what are likely the addresses for both, giving you a choice about whether to reach out to them . . . or not."

"Yes, but . . ." I falter. "Yes, but which address is for which parent?"

"Only you will be able to discover that for yourself. I have done all I can do. You have a week to do some investigating, if you wish to do so. These addresses are not far from here, long walks or rides on the Intra-Rail. They're day trips you can make while still staying here for your last remaining week."

"Okay," I reply, trying to sound optimistic. "Thank you, Sister. I will let you know what choices I make within the next few days."

My head spinning, I get up and leave her office.

Quite the decision to make.

——— o0o ———

Twenty Earth-Standard Years Ago

MY NAME IS MARTIN MILLSTONE. I am one of the very few astronomers and historians living on Prox. And, as a historian, I think it's important everyone know a little bit about where we live.

Prox is a strange planet. Two thousand years ago, the astronomers on Earth determined Proxima Centauri had at least one planet, Proxima Centauri b. I believe back then, they referred to such objects as exoplanets. With their limited instruments, they eventually discovered this planet is 1.2 times the mass of Earth, and it is in what is called the star's "Goldilocks Zone," the distance from the star in which water can exist in all three states—solid, liquid, and gas.

And while the scientists were excited about all of this, they also came to the eventual conclusion this ball of rock was, in all likelihood, tidally locked. That is to say, one hemisphere always faces its sun, and the other hemisphere always faces out into the star-filled void. They also discovered that its sun side receives approximately two thousand times the amount of radiation the earth does, this because its sun, Proxima Centauri, is prone to periodic solar flares. It is one of the more unfortunate aspects of establishing a colony on Prox, the need to protect oneself from solar radiation.

Not ideal conditions, mind you. But curiosity eventually pushed explorers out into the space between the stars. And traveling at 10 percent of the speed of light, Proxima b was the only exoplanet which could be reached within the span of one's lifetime. After years in deep sleep, the first group of people and their collection of ships entered into orbit around our world, carrying everything needed to establish a colony. They found while it was not the perfect place to set up shop, there did exist a zone between the day side of the planet and its night side, a sort of ring running around the entire planet, a ring which had a temperature one could tolerate. There just wasn't a breathable atmosphere.

The explorers made plans to descend to the surface and look around. They brought with them a power plant, a factory capable of 3D-printing, habitation modules, building materials, and tools. Everything necessary to build a small settlement under a dome in the middle of the zone, a place where their sun remained on the horizon all the time. They quickly learned the limitations of their environment. Travel too far into what became known as the Sunside, and things became too hot to tolerate. Travel too far into the Shadeside, and things became mind-numbingly cold.

Despite the less-than-optimal environment, the group had no intention of making the long voyage back to Earth, especially since all of the people the explorers knew back on Earth would be dead. Nor did they wish to spend the rest of their lives aboard their starship. So, they sent a radio message back to Earth, informing them of their discoveries, letting them know no one would be returning, and extending an invitation to any future colonists interested in joining them.

Life went on. The colonists decided to call this world Prox and simply referred to their star as "the sun." It was simpler than saying "Proxima Centauri." With the years came more people from Earth, bringing with them more equipment, building materials, animals which would breed and provide food, fish that could fill the few artificial lakes existing under the Dome, and all variety of seeds for plants, both feed crops and trees and grasses which would help generate more oxygen for the inhabitant's biosphere. The colony grew. And since the land on either side of the Ring could not easily be developed, the colonists moved further and further around the Ring.

Not surprisingly, the growth of their settlement came to a halt when it ran up against mountains at opposite ends of the Dome. Realizing this to be a problem, plans were made to move out into the Shadeside and the Sunside after they discovered a vast network of lava tubes underground, the perfect location for building new living quarters. Over the years, communities spread out into the vicinities on each side of the Ring, and their inhabitants became more and more comfortable with their extreme environments. Eventually, they traveled less and less to the Ring, or the land on the opposite side of the Ring. The skin of people who lived on the Sunside slowly changed to become darker and darker. The increased melanin content in their skin seemed to help them tolerate the heat. And the skin of the people who lived in the Shadeside became paler and paler, perhaps the result of the lower temperature. As the decades and then the centuries passed, the people living at the extreme edges of habitability referred to themselves as either of the Sun or of the Shade.

Oh, yes. One last thing. Given there is no day or night or changing of the seasons, the colonists had to arrive at some way to mark the passage of time. Since Prox circles its sun once every 11.2 Earth-standard days, it was generally agreed 32 cycles would approximately equal one Earth-standard year. But try as the colonists might to arrive at some way to equate Earth-standard time with the reality of Prox's orbital period, they finally gave up and continued to measure time using Earth-standard units.

——— o0o ———

Monday Afternoon

IT'S A BIT EARLY FOR MID-MEAL. The dining room is almost empty. But Jinn is already there, no doubt eager to hear about my meeting with Sister Kaa'thrina. I sit down in my usual seat without getting a tray or any food. I'm not hungry yet.

"So, what happened? What'd you find out?" Jinn pushes his tray aside and gives me his full attention.

"I'm not sure where to start." I take a deep breath, close my eyes, and think about the note one of my parents sent to me. "First of all, my parents might just be alive. So maybe I'm not an orphan after all. Second, there was only one piece of paper in the file the Sister gave me. Here." I hand Jinn the folder.

He opens it and reads the note. "That's it?" he says after reading the note.

"Yep. Sister Kaa'thrina told me it was sent here some time back, presumably by one of my parents. But she's not certain."

"So many questions." Jinn shakes his head from side to side. He scratches his temple for a moment. "Are your parents really still alive? Was it really one of your parents that brought you here? And, if so, which one? And why?" After another minute he adds, "Interesting it gives two addresses. Makes it seem like your parents are no longer together. Maybe someone was trying to hide you from someone else. Perhaps one of your parents was trying to keep you away from the other parent? Or maybe they were both in danger somehow, and they left you here to protect you."

"Sure," I reply. "Any of those things is possible. My folks might well be alive. But the two separate addresses seem to suggest they are no longer together. I wonder whether they were together when I arrived here? I wonder if these addresses are even still current?"

"Good point. So, what are you going to do?" Jinn's eager eyes stare at me.

"I'm not quite sure yet. Assuming I make an effort to visit one or both of my parents . . ." I pause. "I don't know which address goes with which parent. But I guess if I have to choose, I will start with the address in the Shadeside. Work my way from darkness to light, just as the note implies. I will just have to take my chances whichever parent living on the Shadeside is happy to see me after all these years."

Jinn begins to eat his lunch again. The aroma from the stew-of-the-day permeates the dining room.

"One thing I do know," I conclude, "all of this has made me hungry. What's for lunch today?"

————— oOo —————

Sixteen Earth-Standard Years Ago

I AM A FATHER NOW, THOUGH I fear I might not be a very good one. Why would I say that?

One year ago, while I was starting my new position on the Sunside, I returned home to the Ring only to find my wife and baby daughter gone without a trace. My wife and I had been having arguments of late, arguments about my desire to accept a permanent position at the school here on the Sunside, a position which would require us to relocate.

Perhaps because I am dark-skinned and of the Sun, and she is fair-skinned and of the Shade, she didn't want to live in a place where she would be the only one of the Shade. Or maybe she was concerned our daughter, who because of our mixed marriage has light-brown skin, would be different from all of the other children there. I don't know.

But I suspect while these issues caused her some degree of apprehension, I think it more likely she was angry with me, furious with me, in fact. She had become obsessed with a misguided belief I was having an affair with a fellow professor at the school, a female colleague who had been showing me the ropes, as they say. There was no affair, though. Yes, this colleague was of the Sun and intelligent. And yes, she was attractive. But I loved my wife and my daughter. So I endured the increasing verbal abuse and the ever-evolving accusations from my wife, hoping against hope she would calm down, agree to move to the Sunside, and realize such a move would benefit our family.

It didn't take me too long to figure out my wife went to the Shadeside, to her parents. I resisted the urge to make a trip to the Shadeside and talk some sense into her. I had received threats from my father-in-law, vowing physical harm would come my way if I attempted to contact my daughter. And there were threats he would contact my employer and make accusations I had done bad things to my wife and daughter. After a great deal of thought, I decided efforts to speak with my wife in such a hostile environment were not a good idea. It would only serve to reinforce my wife's negative opinion of me, further alienating me from my daughter. So, given a choice between taking several steps backward and standing still, I chose to stand still and have faith everything would eventually work out. I had to become content with searching the information web on Prox to learn about my wife and daughter and how they were doing. Certainly not ideal, but it was better than nothing.

—— o0o ——

Monday Night

ANXIETY GRIPS ME, WAKES ME IN the middle of my sleep cycle. I've been dreaming. The dream begins playing over and over again in my mind. I'm standing in front of a viewing port on a starship, perhaps the ship that brought my ancestors to this world. I look out at all of the stars, don't recognize any of them, and don't know their names. But one of them is particularly bright. An inside voice tells me it is Proxima Centauri. The ship begins to speed up, which I find odd. I had always assumed spaceships must begin to decelerate as they approach their destination. In the next instant I see a planet growing larger. I immediately know it to be Proxima b—Prox. The ship is heading directly for it. Frozen in place, I can only feel the fear of death well up inside me. The ship is going to crash, and I'm going to die. In the next instant, it is over.

But I am not dead. My consciousness has expanded. Half of me feels intense cold, the other half feels burning hot. I am now Prox. The dream ends.

It doesn't take long to decipher the dream's meaning. I am indeed like Prox, with one parent of the Sun and one parent of the Shade. Half of who I am comes from my mother, and the other half comes from my father. Is one half cold and dark, and the other half full of warmth and light? Which is which? Is this really who my parents are, who I am?

TWO

Tuesday Midday

FUNNY THING ABOUT PROX. Because it is tidally locked, there isn't anything one might consider to be day or night, morning or evening. There's just a constant amount of light. How much light is entirely dependent on where you are on the planet. The Abbey where I live is pretty much right in the middle of the Ring, not far from the site of the First Landing Monument. When I step outside after first-meal, it isn't morning or afternoon or evening. It just is. But whenever it is, the air seems fresh and clean, almost invigorating. Because the trees and the grasses receive a steady amount of light, and because the water recycling facilities shower them with brief periods of artificial rain, the plant life is continually producing the oxygen all of us inhabitants need. And what oxygen they don't produce is generated by the electrolysis of water extracted from the permafrost on the Shadeside.

As I look up to my right, there is a gradient of color going from the pale pink overhead to the darkness, almost black at the horizon. I can even make out a few stars. And to my left is another gradient, this one going from the pale pink to the bright red at the opposite horizon. And then there is our sun, Proxima Centauri, resting on the edge of the world, always resting, and never climbing high into the sky like the stories told of the sun on Mother Earth.

The Sisters teach us about Earth and about how our ancestors would speak of things called automobiles. On Prox, we do not have such things, at least not yet. Maybe we will someday. We haven't been here on this planet long enough to reinvent such things or build factories capable of producing such things. And we haven't discovered the hydrocarbon fuels we would need to power such vehicles. We're not there yet. Maybe it's a blessing.

But we have discovered deposits of iron and all sorts of other minerals. And we have learned to reproduce some of the machines which were on Earth. After we expanded into the extreme lands of light and dark, sun and shade, and after the maze of tunnels became more and more settled, the new towns thought it might be a convenient thing to have some sort of rail system. I think the Earthers called them subways.

I set out for the nearest Intra-Rail station after crossing over to the Shadeside. I check my map to make sure I'm heading in the right direction. Once I arrive at the station, I wait for the next Intra-Rail to Bramhall.

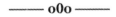

I arrive at the Bramhall address, not knowing what to expect or who it is that might answer the door. My mother? My father? Will I even recognize them as my parent? My nerves are on fire. I force myself to reach for the "call"

button and press it. After a minute or two, the door slides open with a hiss.

"Yes? What do you want? And who are you?" An elderly woman stands in front of me, apparently annoyed at the interruption to her day. She is shorter than me by several centimeters. Her hair is a dirty white and unkempt. She looks haggard, tired, and projects an aura of unhappiness. I can see past her, into the poorly lit recesses of her apartment. Piles of everything imaginable are everywhere. There is no furniture visible, but perhaps some exists under the piles.

"I said, who are you and what do you want!"

I finally manage the only relevant question on my mind. "Are you the mother of Madison Mills?"

"And who wants to know? Are you the police?"

"No, ma'am. I am Madison Mills."

"So. After all of these years, you find your way back to me. Strange twist of fate, eh? How in the world did you find me?"

"I have been raised by the Sisters at the Abbey, the one at the center of the Ring. The Sisters there gave me a note yesterday. They said it was sent to them by one of my parents. There were two addresses listed in the note. One of them was your address. But based on your response, I am to assume the note came from my father."

"Well, then. Did your deadbeat father send you here to harass me, to torment me after he came looking to steal you away from me? Did you know that? Did he make up stories about how horrible of a mother I was?"

"No, ma'am. I have never met my father or spoken with him. I have no memories of you or him."

The woman's face changed from an expression of surprise to one of anger.

"Why are you here? What the hell brings you to my doorstep? Are you looking for a handout? Come to extract some penitence from an old woman who barely can afford food? Or are you looking for some sort of apology?" She pauses to collect her breath, then continues. "Well, you're not getting any money from me, and you're sure as hell not going to get any apology!"

"I didn't come here for money or an apology. I simply came because I wanted to meet the woman who bore me and to understand, perhaps for the first time in my life, how it is I came to be at the Abbey. Up until yesterday, I thought I was an orphan."

"Here I am, child! Are you impressed?" She reaches for the side of the door and leans against it, exhausted from our encounter.

"You should go in and sit down," I suggest. "You seem tired."

"You're damned right, I'm tired! Tired of living a life squirreled away in this dingy little hole, robbed of everything I ever had. And hiding . . . always hiding . . . thanks to your father. But you found me, and I suspect your father won't be far behind."

"I will leave you. I don't mean to upset you or cause you to relive unpleasant memories. But before I go, I need to ask you one question."

"Ask away, child. I might have an answer."

"Okay. If my father really did try to steal me away from you when I was very young, how did I end up at the orphanage? I need to understand."

"Go away. You've had your fun. You've met your mother. I hope you like what you found."

She reaches to the side of the doorway and presses a button. The door slides shut.

—— o0o ——

Twelve Earth-Standard Years Ago

THE HARDEST THING ABOUT BEING a parent is the incessant need to know one's child is happy and healthy. It is especially difficult when there is no communication regarding how one's child is doing. A few years after my wife left for the Shadeside, it became evident to me there would be no reconciliation, no attempts to reach out or give our daughter the opportunity to know her father.

So, I prayed daily, prayed for my daughter's health and well-being. After several years, I made the assumption my daughter was likely in school. I contacted the school closest to my in-law's address to find out how she was doing. Much to my surprise, the school said they had no record of my daughter being enrolled. I thought maybe my wife and my daughter moved, thought maybe my daughter was attending a school in a different neighborhood. But everywhere I checked, there was no record of her.

I eventually hired someone to determine the whereabouts of my daughter. The investigator did confirm my wife had moved to an apartment not far from her parents some years back. After watching my wife's apartment for a week or two, the investigator reported no sign of my daughter. I directed him to check the hospital, the office of the local magistrate, and the public death records. Still nothing.

The investigator did finally come across records suggesting that while the name Madeleine Millstone disappeared, the name Madison Mills appeared around the same time. There was no death record for Madeleine, and there was no birth record for Madison. I never thought my wife would change our daughter's name. The investigator eventually found the whereabouts of my daughter. She had been placed in the orphanage sometime after my wife and daughter left the Ring.

I was grateful to learn of my daughter's location and to know she was being taken care of by the Sisters.

As I step back from all of this with the benefit of hindsight, I wonder if my wife left our daughter at the orphanage because she was unable or unwilling to raise her as a single parent. Maybe she didn't like looking at our daughter and seeing pieces of me. Perhaps she simply wanted to hurt me by denying me the one thing more precious than anything else in my life. I may never know the real reason. But if my wife had wanted to use our daughter to cause me pain, then maybe she and her father might be watching the orphanage, keeping tabs on our daughter. I started to question what might happen if I went to the orphanage and tried to reclaim my daughter, offered to raise her. I recalled the threats of physical harm and thought my contacting the orphanage might put me and my daughter in danger. Maybe it would be best if I left my daughter under the protection of the Sisters.

A difficult decision to make. And I had another decision to make, though not one quite so difficult. Whether to file for a divorce. But I did. And it was uncontested. There was no response to the summons. It was time to put the past behind me and to look forward to a time when we might again connect. I continued to thank the Good Lord for knowledge of my daughter's whereabouts and continued to pray for Madeleine's, or Madison's, happiness and health.

—— oOo ——

Tuesday Afternoon

THE TRIP BACK TO THE ABBEY SEEMS to take longer than my trip to the Shadeside. I was preoccupied with my anxiety earlier and wasn't paying attention to the time. But now, I feel sad, very sad. I feel sad for my mother. And even though I have never met my father, I feel sad for him. And I feel sad for whatever turmoil they must have dealt with all those many years ago. Sadness for whatever would fracture a marriage and a relationship with one's child.

I go straight to my room when I arrive back at the orphanage. I lie down and stare at the ceiling for a good long while. The same thoughts and questions run through my mind over and over again. But I did have one question answered. I now know which address goes with which parent. And maybe tomorrow or the next day, I might set out for the address on the Sunside and meet the man my mother claims is a monster, though I have my doubts. Something deep down inside keeps telling me it is not an accurate description of a man I do not know. After all, it might just be my father found me here and decided I would be better off here than being raised by my mother. After today's meeting, I can't say I blame him. My mother is most definitely not a warm and loving person. But perhaps she was different back then. Who knows?

The dinner bell finally rings, and I get up to wash my hands. Jinn will want a full report. I am so blessed to have such a wonderful friend.

—— oOo ——

Tuesday Evening

"SO?" JINN SAYS WITHOUT EVEN waiting for me to sit down or extend a greeting.

I pull out my chair and try to get comfortable. I stare up at the ceiling for a minute, then lower my gaze, finding Jinn's inquiring eyes.

"I don't know what to say." I am finding all of this harder than I thought. "I was so shocked at her appearance . . . her words . . . her . . . her anger toward me. I couldn't think. She disarmed me. It isn't what I expected, not what I wanted."

Jinn sits quietly, nodding his head in acknowledgment.

"I am so sorry, so very sorry your encounter with your mother didn't go well, that she didn't express some small modicum of joy at meeting you, some small amount of love."

"Thanks, Jinn." I always find his concern for me so comforting.

The sound of clanking plates and silverware from the kitchen fills the dining room. I hang my head down and close my eyes.

"What if my parents are this angry old woman and the monster she claims my father to be?" I feel a tear run down my face. "I'm scared, Jinn. If this truly is the situation, then what does it make me?"

"No, Maddie. You are not an angry person. Nor are you a monster. You are a beautiful ray of sunshine. I should know. I've known you longer than anyone else in your life."

I reach for a napkin and gently wipe my eyes.

"I don't know what to do. What if I go to the other address and find out my father really is a monster. Then what? I have less than one week to figure out what I'm doing when I leave here. I'm reasonably certain I don't want to live with my mother. And I'm certain I can't handle another revelation like the one I experienced today."

"I understand," says Jinn. "But here's what I think you should do right now. You should get up and go to the kitchen. The soup is very good this evening. Get yourself a bowl and get a piece of the bread. The Sisters baked it this afternoon. It's still warm. Then, after dinner, go to your room and get some sleep. We can talk more in the morning."

"Okay," I reply in a quiet voice. "Wise counsel."

——— oOo ———

Wednesday Morning

I'M SITTING IN THE ORPHANAGE library, not reading anything, not completing some final academic assignment before the Sisters allow me to leave. No, all of my school-work is done. I have been a good student, and my teachers have repeatedly praised me, and that makes me feel good, like I've accomplished something in my time here. No, not sure why I'm here. Perhaps I'm just restless.

But I have some decisions to make.

I'm staring out one of the windows, staring out into a part of the terraformed landscape under the Dome, filled with plants of all varieties, all facing toward the Sunside.

What must it have been like to be one of the original explorers? To wake up on a spaceship after decades of deep sleep? To wake up and prepare to descend to the surface of a planet with the pull of gravity again, more gravity than on the spaceship, more gravity than on Earth?

What must it have been like to construct the original section of the Dome? To build the first living quarters, or the oxygen-generating facility, or the water recycling system, or the food processing center? What must it have been like to know that no matter how difficult things might be, no matter how much one might regret one's decision to leave Earth? Their decision was final, and it could never be reversed. You could never go back. I wonder if the original explorers remembered what caused them to leave Earth.

And did any of my ancestors ever have regrets about the decision they made, the decision to come to Prox, to work their whole lives toward a goal they would not see fulfilled, to find peace in knowing their place in the building of a world?

Was there excitement when they discovered the underground system of lava tubes, explored them, and charted them? Records show it took decades to excavate portions of the tunnels, to make additional living quarters, and build the entire underground infrastructures necessary to support the new communities.

What did the colonists living in the extreme places think when, over the course of generations, they found the color of their skin slowly changing, becoming darker or lighter, adapting to their environments? How did people live years underground without ever seeing the sun? How did they deal with always being a little bit too warm or too cool? Not something I could do.

When I think about all of this, I realize how lucky I've been to live in a well-established environment, how lucky I've been to live above ground where I can see the sun, even if it is permanently resting on the horizon.

My life is comfortable because of all those generations of Proxians, everything they did, everything they endured, everything they sacrificed. I'm proud of my forebears, even if I don't know their names.

I try to remember all of this every time I start feeling sad about leaving the orphanage, about not having known my parents. And today, this morning, I think about it again when I reflect on yesterday's meeting with my mother.

My final thought before I get up and return to my room is this: years from now, I do not want to look back at this time and feel regret. I do not want to second-guess the decisions I must now make. Will I do things I should not have done? Will I not do things I should have done? I suppose only time will tell. I must stay strong and keep a clear head.

Should I seek out my father? Do I follow my head or my heart?

Faith, I remind myself. I must have faith the Good Lord will guide me to where it is I am supposed to be. And then, only when the time is right. I am convinced all good things will come to me in the end. And if good things aren't coming to me now, then I must not be at the end.

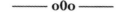

Wednesday Afternoon

LYING ON MY BED, MEDITATING, I GO through my usual mental routine of focusing on each part of my body, releasing whatever tension my mind might find in an arm, or a leg, or my neck, or my back. After completing its physical inventory, my mind goes to a place full of peace. My favorite park or an image of Earth with its wide-open spaces and vast oceans. Despite my fears and concerns about where I will go and what I will be doing four short days from now, I can find some peace. I feel very blessed with the ability to find such serenity in the midst of uncertain circumstances.

After thirty minutes of reveling in my peace, there is a quiet knock on my door.

"Maddie? You awake?" Jinn is trying to be respectful, no doubt. I'm sure he thinks he will be able to slip away if there is no answer. But I push up my inner self through the mists of tranquility.

"I'm meditating," I manage.

"Oh, I'm sorry. I can come back later. Just wondering if you want to go for a walk?"

"No, it's okay. I'm just about ready to get up," I say softly. "How about I get on my walking shoes and meet you downstairs in fifteen minutes?"

"Okay, sounds good. See ya then," Jinn answers. I hear him walk down to the end of the hall and, with careful steps, head down the stairway.

I start my end-of-meditating ritual. "Perfect peace, perfect comfort, perfect health of mind, body, and spirit," I recite this three times, then begin to move my fingers, my hands, my wrists, and then my arms. After a few minutes, I bring one leg at a time up to my chest and give each leg a little hug before releasing it down. I open my eyes and offer a prayer of gratitude before swinging up and off my bed. Walking shoes on, I head down to meet up with Jinn.

We set out into the open air. Jinn's trusty walking stick, which accompanies us on all of our walks, isn't really a stick. A stick would imply it's made from wood. Given the rarity of trees on Prox, it's definitely not wood. Rather, it's a piece of plastic piping, leftover from some construction project Jinn just happened across several years ago.

"How was your meditation, Maddie?" Jinn asks, always so good about asking how my activities were, always so considerate.

"Very peaceful, which I found to be surprising knowing I face some major life decisions in the next few days." We are walking at a fairly good pace, as we usually do. I allow Jinn to choose which of our many walking routes we take.

"But some curious thoughts came to me," I say.

"Oh, yeah? Like what?"

"I was thinking about our lives here. I don't mean at the orphanage. I mean here on Prox. If we are to believe everything we read or learn about Earth, one might conclude we, and I suppose by 'we' I mean the original explorers, gave up an awful lot to come here, to be here."

"Okay. Say more about that."

"One simple example would be wind. Because we live under a climate-controlled dome, because Prox doesn't have much of an atmosphere, and because Prox doesn't rotate, there is no natural or artificial wind."

"That thought never occurred to me, but you're right."

"And there are no sunrises or sunsets, things permeating the literature and art of Earth. And there is no day and no night, no seasons, no oceans or beaches. Do you want me to go on? I just wonder what it would be like to smell salt air and walk along a beach."

A cadence is created by Jinn's walking stick each time it strikes the surface of our path. "I understand. Hmmm, this could get kind of depressing if you dwell on such things for too long."

"I've meant to ask you a question these last few days. It's a rather serious question."

"Ask away. I'm ready,"

"Have you ever thought about leaving Prox? You and me? Neither of us have anyone special here. Though I guess I should wait for a bit before I can be sure. Who knows? If I decide to meet my father and find that he's a good person, that might cause me to stay. I don't know. I'm just thinking out loud here."

"Where would you go? It's not like we can just jump on the Intra-Rail and end up on Earth, or Mars, or Europa, you know?"

"Oh, I know. But I wasn't thinking about going back. The few ships coming to Prox don't go back anymore, if they ever did. No. I'm thinking about heading out to the next world humanity will touch."

We walk in silence for several minutes. I must have given Jinn something to think about, something he had not anticipated.

"You know, there is a ship heading our way. It started its deceleration a few years ago. It's supposed to arrive here in another year or two before heading out to Alpha Centauri A or Alpha Centauri B, I think," I say.

"Look, I do understand your desire to experience the things you mentioned," says Jinn in a thoughtful manner. "But heading out to stars which reportedly have few planets, perhaps planets too close to their sun, or gas giants with questionable moons around them—I'm not so sure there is a high probability of finding a paradise planet with your oceans and beaches and seasons. And then what? Do the travelers go back to sleep for a third time and head out to yet another star system without any guarantees they will find an Earth-like planet? Ross 248? Barnard's Star? How many sleep cycles can a human body endure? How long can a human body tolerate prolonged sleep, anyway?"

"I see your point," I say, agreeing with Jinn's concern. "So does that mean we'll never experience wind or waves, or a sky full of daylight, or a breathtaking sunset?"

"Well, I'm just saying there's no good way to find those things without significant sacrifice. Maybe it's a matter of perspective. It might just be we should count our blessings, be content with what we do have, here, now. You might find your father to be an amazing and loving person. And who knows what's in my file? I might find I, too, have parents or relatives who would be willing to take me in and get me started on whatever line of work fate has in store for me. We just don't know yet."

"You're probably right. What you're saying makes sense. I'm just taking this moment in my life to question everything."

"I know, and that's okay," says Jinn in a sympathetic voice.

We arrive at the park we often circumnavigate. Jinn chooses to walk counterclockwise around it today. It is one of the few places on Prox with trees and an open body of water. There are even a few fish swimming around in it. All species of flora and fauna were brought from Earth, or at least, their DNA was.

As we hit the halfway point in our walk, Jinn says something I find unexpected, even uncharacteristic for the Jinn I have come to know all of these years. "You know, Maddie, you've been talking about heading out in the plural. You said 'we' several times. Am I to assume you meant we would make the journey together?"

"Yes, I suppose I did say that, didn't I? It's because I can't imagine life without you in it. I know it probably sounds a bit serious, but it is the truth, Jinn. You are the most important thing, the most important person, in my life."

We walk for ten minutes without any further conversation and complete our circumnavigation of the park before heading back to the orphanage.

"Jinn," I finally say in an apologetic voice, "I'm sorry if I said anything to upset you. I don't want you to think I'm seriously contemplating running off to the stars without you. I could never do that."

Jinn turns his head toward me and says in what is almost a whisper, "I know." The smile on his face brings back the feeling of peace I had during my meditation. I smile back.

THREE

Thursday Afternoon

WE ARE SITTING BACK IN THE dining room at our usual table. Other residents have finished eating and returned to their rooms or the library or wherever they were before the midday meal. Jinn and I have barely spoken.

"Jinn," I finally say, hoping he will look up from his tray. "I have made a decision and I want to share it with you and my thinking behind it."

Jinn's blue eyes find me. "Okay. You know I'm listening. Go ahead."

"Thanks," I acknowledge. "I've decided to go and see my mother again."

"Really? I'm curious why you would do that before trying to find your father."

"Good question," I agree. I shift my weight in my chair. "Some things just don't seem right about my mother's response to meeting me . . . and I mean the grown-up me, of course. First of all, now that I know at least one of my parents is alive . . . and perhaps they both are . . . one of them must have put me in this orphanage. When I asked her how I ended up at the orphanage, she told me to go away. She didn't answer the question. That doesn't make any sense. Second, my mother asked me if I was looking for an apology from her. Except I can't quite figure out why I would expect an apology. An apology for what? It almost seems like she was the one who left me here. And if she did, I want to know why."

"Okay. I'm with you. Keep going," interjected Jinn.

"And then there was her anger. Why would she be so angry at me for seeking her out? It almost seems like she didn't want me to find her. And why would that be? If my father placed me here against her wishes, wouldn't she be just at least a little bit glad that I sought her out? I don't know. I guess I have lots of questions I would like her to answer. Based on my first visit, I'm not certain I will get very far. But if my father really is a bad person and he really did do something bad to my mother, I'd like to know more about what happened all those years ago and which parent put me here before I go traipsing off to find my father. I want to be prepared to deal with whatever I find."

"Okay, I follow your thinking." Jinn looks out the window for a moment, then returns his gaze to me. "Would you like me to go with you? I don't mean to suggest I would go in with you, if that even happens. Your mother wouldn't even have to know I'm there. I'm happy to wait outside. That way, you don't have to make the trip back here by yourself."

"That's very sweet of you, Jinn." Relieved, I accept his offer.

Another smile crosses Jinn's wonderful face. "When are you thinking about going. There's not a lot of time left for you here."

"I know. Don't remind me. Let's head out tomorrow morning after first-meal. That should get us back with enough time for me to meet again with Sister Kaa'thrina. She's been so good to me over the years. On Saturday, I want to save for packing up my few possessions and saying goodbye to everyone else here."

"And your father? What about him?"

"I don't know yet. Let's see how tomorrow goes, okay?"

—— o0o ——

Friday Morning

"SO. YOU DECIDED TO PAY ME another visit, did you?" says my mother as the door slides open. "You've got some courage, I'll say that. Wonder which side of the family that comes from, eh?"

I'm immediately taken aback. She is presenting a much different picture of herself. Perhaps she was expecting another visit and cleaned herself up? Her hair is brushed and pulled back in a bun. Her clothes seem less drab. And maybe it's my imagination, but she seems to be wearing some makeup.

"Well, don't just stand there. Come in," she offers me an unanticipated invitation. I am shocked at the change of her demeanor.

"Thank you," I reply. As I move through the doorway, I am surprised to see a much different living space. Gone are the piles of clutter. The room is lighter. There are pictures and paintings on the wall and pieces of furniture. And there is an aroma of something cooking in the kitchen.

"So," she starts off again. "Let me guess. You have questions. You want to know more about me and your father, how we met, and why we parted ways. Hmmm. You might be surprised to know I have some questions for you."

You better believe I have some questions, I think to myself. *Like which one of my parents placed me in the orphanage.* But I keep silent for now.

She motions me to sit down in a chair covered with featureless material. Fabric produced on Prox doesn't generally have ornate patterns or intricate textures. "Please, ask me anything you like," I offer.

My mother crosses the small living room and sits herself down into a matching chair. She takes a sip of water from a glass sitting on a three-legged table next to her seat. She clears her throat and begins.

"How did you find me, again? You said your father sent you a note?"

I need to be careful, I think. I shouldn't offer too much information until I'm sure of her intentions. "You might know I'm getting ready to turn eighteen on Monday, as a matter of fact. The orphanage . . . that is where I've been living my whole life . . . ends their care for kids when we turn eighteen. My time there is almost up."

My mother is staring rather intently at me. It makes me feel uncomfortable.

"To help prepare us for the outside world, the orphanage shares any information they might have on who brought us there and when and any other information they might have about our background. They also give us any names of individuals who might put us up or help us find work once we leave the orphanage."

She continues to stare. I wonder what she is thinking. At least she is listening. Listening and not yelling or screaming at me.

"Earlier this week I met with the Sister who has been responsible for me my entire life, Sister Kaa'thrina. She gave me a file. There was only a single piece of paper in the file. The paper didn't say much. But what the Sister did say is she thought the note was from one of my parents. She just didn't know which one. And the note gave two addresses. One on the Shadeside, which is how I found you, and the other address is for the Sunside, an address I have yet to visit. You should know the note did not say which address went with which parent. The fact I'm reaching out to you first is simply the luck of the draw."

"That's a nice story," my mother says. She is twitching about nervously. "What address did your father leave for himself?"

"I don't recall the exact address, and I didn't bring the note with me. But I do seem to recall the address is somewhere in Alphatown. I have no way of knowing whether it is still a good address. I'm trying to decide whether I want to visit him. Based on your description of him, he doesn't seem to be a very nice person."

"No, he is not. He hurt me, young lady. Hurt me real bad . . . really, really bad." She appears anxious. She clenches a fist and then relaxes it. "He hurt me so much. I wanted to hurt him back. Get revenge, you know?"

"Revenge? For what?" I inquire.

"For having an affair, an affair with another woman. Someone of the Sun. Someone like himself. You do know your father is of the Sun, don't you?" There is bitterness in her voice.

"After meeting you several days ago, seeing you were of the Shade, I assumed he must have been. I mean, look at me and my skin color and my hair color. I'm obviously not of the Sun or of the Shade."

"Yes. I suppose you might have come to that conclusion."

"But you mentioned you wanted to hurt him back, to extract some sort of revenge. Tell me more about that." I stop for a moment, then add, "I'm thinking if you didn't physically hurt him, hit him or beat him, maybe you might strike out at something important to him, spread untruths about him. Maybe make some sort of false accusation by saying he had done something wrong when he didn't. Is that what you mean?"

"I see you have an active imagination. You've done some thinking about this, have you?"

I nodded my head in agreement. "Yes. Now that you mention it."

"Good, good. What would you say if I told you I took from your father the one thing he loved more than anything else in this crumby ol' world?"

My mind starts racing. I bite my lip, hesitant to ask the inevitable question. "And what might that be?"

"You, my dear. You."

"What do you mean?"

"Your father was going to move to the Sunside and take you with him. To be fair, take us with him. Though why he would want me there when he was having an affair with this other woman, I don't know."

"Okay. I'm still not getting it."

"Your father was making periodic trips to the Sunside to go to the new position he started. One time, while he was gone, I took you to the Shadeside. We went to stay with my parents. But I knew when your father returned the next time, he would wonder where we were. Sooner or later, he would conclude I left him and took you with me . . . and that we were with my parents. So, I decided to hide you, to take away the one thing he would want."

My body starts to tremble. I'm not able to believe what it is I am hearing.

"You see? I'm the one who took you to the orphanage. I'm the one who left you there. I left only a small note wrapped up in your blanket. It simply said, 'my name is Madison Mills.' But that is not your birth name, my dear. No. Your name was Madeleine Millstone. I thought by changing your name, your father would never find you. But apparently, at some point, he did figure out what I had done."

My mother goes on. "It was for your own good, you know? I knew if your father found me, he would have taken you. And then what? I did it to protect you. The man was a monster, probably still is." My mother pauses to catch her breath. "Based on what you've told me, he apparently sent you a note. I'm curious. Did he use your birth name or the new name I gave you?"

I don't answer the question even though I know the answer. My father did not use my birth name, perhaps out of respect for me, or maybe out of some respect for my mother. I'm not sure why. I can't think of any reason why he would do anything else.

"Let me get this straight. You left me at the orphanage just to hurt my father?" My mind is struggling to process all of this. Finally, I blurt out, "And you have the nerve to call my father a monster? I'm sorry. It seems to me you are the monster here."

I stand up. I face my mother and say, "I am so glad I finally know the truth. I am choosing never to see you again. Goodbye, mother."

I find the button to open the door and head out to find Jinn. I'm so glad he came with me.

——— oOo ———

Saturday Evening

AFTER WE FINISH OUR DINNER together, Jinn proposes we head out to the back of the Abbey. There is a nice little brick patio offering a glorious view of the dark side of the sky. We find ourselves two chairs and settle in for what Jinn calls "a sit."

Minutes tick by. We watch the procession of stars as they cross the black sky. I lean back in my chair and tilt my head up. Jinn points out Earth's sun, Sol, a bright yellow star shining just under Cassiopeia's easily recognizable "W."

I break the quiet of the evening. "It's been over a thousand years since humans arrived here. You would think we could have created a better world than the one our forefathers left so long ago. But no. Hatred and anger and a need for revenge have followed us as we've spread out into the stars. Perhaps such negative emotions are not things we can leave behind as we move on. Perhaps it is because they are part of us, and no matter how hard we try, we will never be able to purge them from our lives." And then I add without giving any forethought, "Why did God create us this way? If we are truly created in the image of God, then is God full of anger and hatred, as well?"

Jinn sits staring off into space. He turns his head to look at me and says, "Maybe God created us to serve as vessels for His anger. Maybe anger is like water, something that can be poured from one vessel to another, leaving the first vessel empty and free of negative emotion."

"Perhaps. But I often wonder if He really punishes those full of anger and really sends good people to heaven when they die. Because if He doesn't, makes you wonder why we even try to clean up our respective acts, why we try to be better people."

Jinn catches me a bit off guard. "Do you ever think maybe your father is looking up at these very same stars at this very same moment?"

I take a deep breathe in and sigh. "No, Jinn. I can't say I have. But I like the thought."

And he offers up a second question to me. "Do you ever think maybe he is saying prayers for you, maybe right now? You know, if I were a parent, and if I had a child from whom I'm separated, I would be praying on them each and every day."

I can't seem to find any words appropriate for his query.

Jinn goes on. "It's been seventeen years since your mother left you here . . . years by Earth counting, of course. Do you realize that works out to be over six thousand Earth-standard days? If your father offers up prayers for you twice a day, that's a whole lot of prayers being directed your way. That makes you one special person."

"You know, Jinn," I start off, "you have an interesting way of thinking about things. I'm not certain I would have come up with either of those thoughts. They are both wonderfully positive, hopeful thoughts. They are thoughts I will take with me when I leave this place on Monday."

"After my time to leave here comes, we will have to find some new places to walk and talk and share meals and sit and watch the sky. I hope we don't live too far apart from one another. I hope our schedules will give us time to do these things we love to do together."

"I do, too," I reply. "I do, too."

———— o0o ————

Sunday Morning

THE WORDS OF MY MOTHER TUMBLE around in my mind during my entire sleep cycle. I finally decide to open my eyes, surprised I don't feel more tired, more hopeless, and more uncertain about tomorrow and where I should go. For some reason, though, I don't feel the severity of the burden I'm facing.

I roll over onto my back as I always do when I say my morning prayers. I give thanks for the new day, for Jinn, for my health, and for the relative abundance with which I am blessed. I give thanks for my skills and my talents. I pray for the Sisters, for the other children here at the orphanage, and for my parents. My old prayer asked God for some hint about whether my parents were still alive, but such a petition no longer seems appropriate. So, I change the words. My new prayer is for a chance to meet my father. And I pray the anger my mother holds on to will leave her. And I always end with a prayer for peace, then take three deep breaths, and release all of my concerns to the Light.

My eyes are closed again. I catch myself drifting back to sleep and grudgingly force myself up into an upright position. I look at my desk and notice the file Sister Kaa'thrina gave me is gone, and in an instant, all of the peace and serenity my prayers brought me evaporates.

As fast as I can, I pull on clothes, run down the hall, and burst through the door separating the girls' rooms from the boys' rooms. Jinn's room is the second door on the left. I immediately start banging on his door.

"It's unlocked!" he shouts with a hint of sleep still in his voice.

"Yes! I know! But I wanted to give some warning before I come inside."

"Come in, Maddie. What in the world is happening?" he says with less sleep in his response. I sit down at the end of his bed.

"The file! It's gone!"

"Do you mean the file Sister Kaa'thrina gave you?"

"Yes! Of course, I do!"

"Are you certain you just didn't misplace it? Maybe you were sleepwalking?"

"No! I know what I did, and I know where I put it before turning in."

"Okay. But at least you know what it said, right?"

I shake my head rather vigorously. "But that's just it! I don't remember the second address, the address for my father. I'm not worried about my mother's address. Once I've been somewhere, I remember how to get there again. But my father? I've never been to his address. I've never even been to the Sunside."

"Okay. Calm down. We'll figure this out," Jinn says in his most comforting tone. He sits up in his bed and pushes his blanket down to his waist. "Maybe Sister Kaa'thrina has another copy. We can go to her office after she gets out of morning prayers."

"Ol' right. Good idea," I say, trying to release some of my anxiety. "But there is another issue, a bigger issue, perhaps. Who would have come into my room in the middle of our sleep cycle and taken the folder? There are only two other people who even knew of its existence."

"Don't you mean three? Sister Kaa'thrina, me, and

your mother." Jinn reminds me. "And since I didn't do it, it leaves either the good Sister or your mother."

"You know, I have always felt a bit uneasy about the fact the orphanage has no locks on any of its doors. If it was my mother, then perhaps she came looking for my father's address. I told her I had it and that means she could now have it."

Jinn stretches out his arms and says, "Makes me wonder if she won't try to get to your father before you do. Maybe even try to cause him harm. We need to warn him, Maddie."

"You're right. Lemme go put on some proper clothes. I'll meet you downstairs in a few minutes."

"Got it. And Maddie, I'm really sorry about all of this."

"I know. Thanks."

JINN AND I GET DOWNSTAIRS AT the same time. "I see some of the Sisters in the kitchen. Morning prayers must be over," says Jinn. "Let's go check out her office."

The two of us head down the south hall where the Sisters have their offices. When we arrive, Sister Kaa'thrina is sitting with her back to us shaking her head from side to side.

"Excuse us, Sister Kaa'thrina," I say. "Are you all right?"

"Someone's been in my office," she sighs. "The file drawers were left open and things on my desk are out of order. Nothing like this has ever happened here before."

"And someone was in my room while I slept," I report.

The Sister turns around to face me and says, "What? How do you know?"

"Because the file you gave me on Monday . . . the file with the addresses of my parents . . . it's gone! And the worst part about it is, I don't remember the address for my father! I only remember he lives on the Sunside, in Alphatown, I think."

"I'm so sorry, child," she says, trying to console me. "Do you have any idea who might have done this?"

Jinn speaks up. "There are only three people besides Maddie who even knew of the file's existence. You, me, and Maddie's mother."

"What in the world would Madison's mother want with the file?"

"My father's address," I reply. "I mentioned I had it when I went to see her a second time on Thursday afternoon. And based on the story she told me about my father, what a monster he was, and how he hurt her, I would think she might be looking to exact some sort of revenge on him. What is the old adage, hell hath no fury like a woman scorned? She believes my father had an affair with another woman. I'm not certain what to do about any of this."

Jinn speaks up a second time. "You wouldn't happen to have another copy of the report you gave Maddie, would you? Or perhaps have her father's address written down somewhere else in your records?"

Sister Kaa'thrina straightens out her desk chair and sits down. She looks at me and shakes her head. "No. I'm sorry. I don't. I just can't believe this is happening. You poor dear."

The three of us stare at one another, none of us knowing what to do.

"I do have one thought, Madison. Tomorrow is your birthday. And I'm certain you recall the small container with the time-lock given to you on your sixth birthday. It should open up for you, perhaps at midnight, tonight.

Based on everything that's happened and everything you have learned about your mother and her apparent need for revenge, I'll just bet there is a good chance it was your father who left the container for you. And if he did, maybe he will include his current address in whatever message he has for you. And if his current address is different from the address in the missing note, your mother shouldn't be able to find him."

"Okay. Good idea. Makes sense," I say, finding some enthusiasm for the first time today. Jinn looks at me and flashes his two thumbs up sign. "So, all we have to do is wait. I will finish packing up my things and saying my goodbyes today. And then at midnight, with any luck, I will have a message from my father. Tomorrow I will set out to pay him a visit."

Sister Kaa'thrina nods her head in agreement. "I know this is a difficult scenario for you, my dear. If you need a few extra nights here until things get sorted out, I'm sure we can accommodate you. I will speak to the Mother Superior about this situation. She'll know what to do."

"Thank you, Sister. You are most kind." I look over at Jinn and say, "Okay. Now I'm hungry. Let's go and get some breakfast."

FOUR

Sunday Night

AT MIDNIGHT, A SLIGHT HISS ESCAPES from the stainless-steel container as the time-lock releases its grip. Inside is a small device. Its only two visible features are an on-off switch and something resembling a little speaker. After years of waiting, I will finally hear words, in all probability, my father recorded for me. All I have to do is press the miniature button.

I hesitate, as if to double-check all of the questions dancing around in my head and in my heart, the same questions I have asked over and over again for the last seventeen plus years, and all of the conclusions I've reached, whether they be correct or not. I make my decision. I will listen to the message and accept the fact the words will affect my life.

I press the play button. In a low volume, the message begins.

Dearest Madison,

Today you are turning eighteen years of age. I wish I could celebrate this day with you. But now that you are becoming aware of events that occurred when you were only an infant, you quite probably have a lot of questions, and quite likely, a lot of anger toward the two individuals who brought you into this world, and I am one of them. For that, I am so very sorry. I will try to keep this short. But it's my hope my words will help you understand why things happened the way they did. After you hear them, my prayer is that you will decide to seek me out. I can give you a more detailed account, then.

By now, you probably know your mother is of the Shade, and you might have concluded I am of the Sun. Folks from the opposite halves of our world don't usually have opportunities to meet and marry. But, as fate would have it, my parents lived in the Ring, where I was born and spent the first twenty-plus years of my life. When they returned to live on the Sunside, I elected to stay in the Ring. Your mother's story is much the same, except her parents were of the Shade and living in the Ring, as well.

After we each finished our schooling, we worked together at the same place for a short time. Your mother changed jobs, but we stayed in contact and eventually fell in love. We married and spent our first few years living in the Ring. Eventually, your mother became pregnant and after a difficult pregnancy, you were born. Thank goodness, you were healthy.

When you were several months old, I was presented with an offer from the school on the Sunside. It was a very good offer, I might add. And since your mother and I planned to have another child, I figured the new position, and the increased compensation would allow your mother to spend the first few years of your life at home taking care of you and your future sibling.

I wanted to be sure the position would be a good fit for me, so I accepted the offer on a tentative basis and started spending the weeks on the Sunside, returning to the Ring on the weekends. Things were going well, so I began searching for a place to live. One of my female colleagues offered to help by showing me around the Sunside.

As the weeks went by, I would return home every weekend to find your mother becoming more and more opposed to the move. If it hadn't been for the fact that the position would give us the means to grow our family, I probably would have turned down the offer and stayed in the Ring. But opportunities like this are difficult to find on Prox. I tried convincing your mother to move, but she finally informed me she would not move, and that you would be staying with her.

I wasn't sure what to do at this point. But I continued commuting to the Sunside every week for several more weeks. Then one evening while I was away, she called me and accused me of having an affair with my female colleague. Because this wasn't true, I tried convincing her such assumptions were wrong.

After I finished teaching my class the next morning, I made the long ride on the Intra-Rail home, only to find she and you were gone. There was no note; no indication where you went. But her clothes and personal things were gone, and all of your clothes and things were gone, as well.

As I tried to come up with some sort of a plan for what to do, one thought came to my mind over and again. This was not the woman I thought I married. I knew our relationship had suffered permanent damage. There would be no peace for any of us from this point on.

You were to be raised by someone full of anger. You were then, and still are, the most precious thing in the world to me. That's when I decided to make every effort to find you, and that's when I started receiving threats from your mother's father, threats to stay away from you. I hired someone to look into your mother's whereabouts . . . and yours. You've probably figured out I did eventually determine where your mother went. And you probably now know I found out she left you at the orphanage several weeks later. I can only assume she did it to hurt me, to keep you from me. And I figured if I came to claim you and take you to live on the Sunside, your mother and her father would find us, sooner or later, and who knows what they might have done to me and, more importantly, to you. I knew the Sisters at the orphanage would tend to your physical and, hopefully, your emotional and spiritual needs until you reached eighteen years old.

So, there you have it. It is a very sad story for each of us. And I am so very sorry things are as they are. It is my sincere hope you, one day, find it in your heart to forgive me and seek me out. If you have already met your mother, I will simply say this: I am not a bad person, or the monster your mother, no doubt, makes me out to be.

One last thing. Several years after I finally moved to the Sunside, I met a wonderful woman, also someone of the Sun. We eventually got married and two years later, we had a little girl. That's right, Madison. You have a baby sister. Her name is Maera Millstone. I so wish you might meet her someday and be a big sister to her, help her to grow and to love life. She is a delight, just as you were, just as you, no doubt, are.

I think this message has gone on long enough. I pray you are well. I pray you will find your way out into the world and become a success at whatever you choose to do in your life. May the Good Lord bless you and keep you.

> *All of my love to you,*
> *Your Father*
> *426 University Place, Sunside*

———— o0o ————

Monday Morning

"A WEEK AGO, WHEN THIS JOURNEY, or whatever you want to call it, started . . ." I take a deep breath, then continue, ". . . I wondered if one of my parents might be some angelic creature who could do no wrong and perhaps my other parent might be some fire-breathing dragon. I'm not sure I know why, but I thought maybe my mother was the angel and my father was the dragon. Now that I've met my mother and heard the note from my father and started to learn what really happened all those many years ago, I'm pretty certain the reverse is true."

Jinn is sitting across the table watching me, no doubt

trying to imagine what sort of agony I am feeling. He has been with me for so many years, knows my hopes and dreams, and is willing to share these discoveries with me. I know he is so wishing things had turned out differently. I look up. "And now, if I am to have a relationship with my father, I must set those beliefs aside, let them go."

Jinn stands up and moves his chair around to my side of the table. He turns his head to face me and says, "Something happened since we spoke at dinner last evening, didn't it? The time capsule? It opened up?"

"Oh, yes," I say in a low voice. "Last night . . . I was still awake. I couldn't sleep. I was too worried about today and leaving this place, leaving you, and not knowing where I will go."

"Very understandable," interrupts Jinn.

"So, at the stroke of midnight, the time capsule lets out a subtle hiss and proceeds to open."

"Really? What was inside?" queries Jinn. He cocks his head to one side.

"There was a small recording device . . ."

"I'm to assume there was a message on the device. Did you listen to it?"

"There was and I did." My voice cracks a bit. I stop to get my emotions in check. "It was a message from my father."

"Oh, wow."

"Oh, wow is right," I say. I open up my right hand and show Jinn the device. I click the on-off button, and we listen to the message.

After it ends, there is a silence. Jinn moves his chair back a few feet and stretches out his long legs. He brings his left hand up to his chin and closes his eyes.

"They're all gone now," I say. "The questions, the wondering why things happened the way they did."

I feel empty inside, an emptiness I have never felt before, an emptiness I never knew could exist. It isn't fair. I didn't do anything wrong. No, this terrible feeling was the fault of my mother, a mother who wanted to use me as a weapon to cause my father pain, to cause a good man pain. And she did it without realizing what it would one day do to me. I suppose I could blame my father for some of this. Maybe he could have sacrificed the position on the Sunside. But I understand his need to provide for us, to accept the new responsibilities which would generate the means to support a growing family. But I do not understand why my mother was so adamantly against moving to the Sunside. Was it something physical? Was it about the greater temperature there? Or was it something else? Was it about being of the Shade and fair-skinned? Did she not want to live in a place where she would be surrounded by people who were dark-skinned and of the Sun?

Jinn and I sit quietly together for a long while as an artificial rain cycle starts outside. The faint sounds coming from the drops as they hit the metal roof above our heads feels appropriate. The heavens are crying just as I am crying.

"You know? My parents are like Prox. Half the sky is light, and half the sky is dark. One parent is of the Sun, and one parent is of the Shade. But I suppose we are all like that inside, I mean. We each have our light side, and we each have our dark side. It's like that for me. Now that I know the truth about my father and my mother."

There are tears in my eyes. Jinn notices and reaches out with his right hand, placing it on my hands. "It will be all right. I will stay with you. Together we will find what is good in this world. Maybe together, we can build something, something which will cover up all of this pain and loss."

I love Jinn and I think Jinn loves me. And not just in some platonic way, but in some way much more, much deeper.

Monday Afternoon

MY NAME IS MADISON MILLSTONE. I am no longer an orphan. I have found my mother. I have found my father, as well, and I think he will be overjoyed when I meet him later today. We will learn about each other. We will make up for the time we have both lost. We will both learn to forgive my mother and pray for her soul. And I have a little sister. And I have Jinn. It will be all right again. I know it will.

Thank you, God.

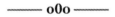

"For God commanded, saying, honour thy father and mother: and he that curseth father or mother, let him die the death."
—Matthew 15:4

THE WISHBRINGER

(The Farmer and the Fantasy)

. . . .

ONE

THE SHIMMER OF THE INTER-dimensional portal began to fade as the reporter set his feet onto solid ground. His first look at the landscape around him revealed fields with rows of bushes and small trees off to his left and his right. *The UX-12 probe was correct*, he thought. *This plane of existence is truly a paradise.*

A dirt road shot out before him and headed straight for what appeared to be a barn and a country-style home. Curious to see who lived there and who tended the fields of unidentifiable crops, he started walking toward the buildings. Some sort of gentle background sound permeated the air, something like the song created by thousands of cicadas mixed with wind chimes, only more subtle, more welcoming.

The front door opened as soon as he entered the yard between the house and the barn. A middle-aged man dressed in overalls and sporting a red bandanna wrapped around a head full of graying hair stepped out onto the front porch. Flashing a broad smile, he seemed to be a friendly sort of fellow.

"Good morning to ya," the man called out.

The reporter replied with a wave and greeting of his own.

"What brings ya to these parts?" continued the man, now making his way down the steps into the yard.

"Jonathan Argent is my name," said the reporter, moving toward the man and extending his right hand. "I'm from the *New Earth News* on planet Earth. I was told you would be expecting me."

"And that I am. Pleasure to meet ya."

"Am I to assume you received our earlier message? My apologies it was not delivered in person, but we never know about the conditions on the other side of the portal when we send out our probes. We want to make sure the atmosphere and temperature of each new realm supports life."

"Oh, I got yer message all right. Must say I was quite surprised. I don't get many visitors here, certainly not from Earth. And I only see a handful of other folks here with any degree of regularity. But come on up to the front porch and have a sit. We can have ourselves a little chat there. My morning chores are done, and I have some time for ya."

The two men found their way up the steps and settled into comfortable rocking chairs, each with a colorful cushion. The farmer set his rocker in motion with a push of his foot.

"Tell me about yourself," said the reporter to start the conversation. "And tell me about this place. It's beautiful. I have to admit we were most surprised to stumble over your niche of the multiverse."

"Yep. Beautiful, it is," remarked the man.

"I'm sorry," said the reporter. "I didn't catch your name."

"Hmmm . . . well . . . I don't really have a name per se. My acquaintances just call me 'the farmer'."

"Ol' righty then, farmer. What do you do here? I see your fields full of a crop I don't recognize. What exactly do you grow here, anyway?"

The farmer smiled and gave a little laugh. "Ah, yes. That is the question, isn't it?" He shifted his body in his rocker, returned his gaze to his interrogator, and simply said, "Wishes."

"Excuse me?" The reporter's sandy-blond eyebrows frowned. "Wishes? How does one grow wishes?"

"Well, in its simplest terms, every morning my friend, Gabriel, arrives here with his pickup truck full of wishes from the people of Earth. Earth? That's where ya said ya was from, wasn't it? Sorry. Meant to say that's what the message I received said."

"That's right, Earth," replied the reporter.

"Okay. So, Gabriel unloads the wishes here in the barnyard. I sort through all of the wishes, categorize them, and head off to the appropriate field to plant them."

"Categorize them? What do you mean?"

"Most wishes sent here have to do with one of four things. They're either about health, wealth, love, or life."

The reporter thought for a moment and silently nodded his head up and down.

The farmer continued. "Over the years, I have found certain wishes grow best in certain fields. It might have something to do with the soil. Not sure, really. The celestial rains come every so often, usually in the afternoon. The wishes grow until they are ready to be harvested. When the time is right, I head out, pick the fruit, and bring it back here to the barnyard where I crate up everything. Then, every afternoon, Raphael or Jophiel or maybe even Cameal sometimes, arrive here to pick up the crates. I'm to assume they then head off to Earth to deliver the wishes to the appropriate wisher."

"Seriously?" said the reporter, not quite certain what to believe. "I never thought about wishes as being things requiring planting or growing or harvesting. This just doesn't seem to make much sense where I come from. I'll have to think about this."

"Well, ya just go ahead and ponder away. From the looks of the dust cloud off in the distance, I think Gabriel is on his way with another load of wishes. Yer welcome to stick around and watch the unloading."

The reporter shook his head affirmatively and said, "I'd be happy to."

Ten minutes later, an old red pickup truck pulled into the yard and the dust slowly settled. The farmer walked out to greet his friend. The reporter watched as the two men exchanged pleasantries and then went around to the back of the truck. Gabriel uncoupled the back gate, and the farmer reached in to grab several of the crates. The reporter was astonished the crates didn't seem to weigh much. Some of them even seemed to glow. After about a dozen trips back and forth to the barn, the men shook hands again. Gabriel climbed back into the truck. The truck made a wide U-turn, headed out of the courtyard and back up the road.

The reporter got up to make his way over to the farmer as he shut the big door to the barn. He asked, "Those crates you just unloaded. They seemed light. How much do they weigh?"

"Oh, not much," replied the farmer. "Wishes are very tiny things when they first arrive. The wishers might not even know they've made the wish. But they're not always like that. There are days when the loads are much heavier. Those wishes are usually for things of much more significance, and dare I say, even life-threatening."

"Okay. Thank you," said the reporter. "And was it my imagination? Did some of the wishes glow?"

"Yep. They do that sometimes. And every once in a while, at night," the farmer pointed out toward the fields, "the more mature plants give off light. Something to see, really."

The farmer led the reporter back up to the front porch where the two of them reclaimed their rocking chairs. The reporter continued his interview.

"You mentioned needing to sort the wishes before you head out to plant. And you said wishes usually come in one of four categories . . . health, wealth, love, and life. I'm wondering if you might say more about this."

The farmer continued rocking. "That's right. Think about it. Most folks want their sickness cured, or they want more money to pay their bills, or they're looking for someone with whom to share their life because they don't want to be alone, or they want some circumstance in their life to change. Perhaps they want a new job, or they want to be relieved of a particular burden, some responsibility. Is this all making sense to ya?"

"Yes. I'm getting it. So, you plant these wishes in their respective fields and they grow until they are ready to be harvested. Then you pick them and send them off to the appropriate wisher." After a pause, the reporter continued, "And just exactly how long does it take for these wishes to grow and mature?"

"Well, now. It depends." The farmer looked up at the sky. "Some wishes grow rather quickly. Some take years to develop. Some never grow at all. It's not uncommon for me to find wishes dead on the branches, just hanging there all withered."

"And you take care of all these crops all by yourself?"

"That I do," said the farmer.

"How's that even possible?" asked the reporter.

"Well, because I have lots of time to do my chores, ya see? No matter how long ya stay here, yer gonna find almost no time has passed when ya get home. Each dimension has its own distinct flow of time."

Clouds started to gather on the far horizon, inching their way toward the westering sun. The farmer returned his gaze to the sky before announcing to his guest, "I think it's time for ya to head back to yer own dimension. A storm is on its way, and we do not want ya to have any difficulties with the dimensional portal. Tell ya what, though. Ya can come back another day. Just don't do it during a storm. Ya got lucky today. Oh, yes, ya did."

"Thanks for the heads up. I am not a fan of all this dimension-hopping. But if it helps to sell stories for the newspaper, then that's what I have to do to put food on the table."

The reporter stood up, bent over to shake hands with his host, and turned to head down the steps. After a quick wave, he walked back up the road to the spot where he had first appeared and activated his portable dimensional transport device. A moment later, the shimmering portal appeared. He stepped through it and vanished.

—— o0o ——

A couple of days later, the reporter returned for a second visit with the farmer via the inter-dimensional portal. He repeated his ritual from the previous visit. Except this time, he first looked at the sky to confirm what the UX–12 probe had communicated back to Earth several minutes earlier. No storm clouds. He set off for the farmhouse and found the farmer waiting for him on the front porch.

After a handshake, the two men sat down in the rockers, and the reporter resumed his questioning.

"First, let me just say how much I appreciate you taking time out of your busy schedule to meet with me. I think the folks back on Earth will be fascinated to learn the wishes they so innocently send out into the universe have a physical form somewhere, that they are nurtured and, perhaps, returned to them."

"My pleasure," said the farmer. "I was told there might be a day when humankind would develop the technology allowing him to learn how the universe really works. Amazing place, this universe, ya know? The Good Lord did a truly remarkable job designing the whole thing, dontcha think?"

"Oh, yes. And ironic you would comment about how it is the universe works. I wanted to start by asking how long you have been here, how long have you been in charge of growing our wishes, for lack of a better way to phrase it?"

The farmer looked to be mentally adding up a long series of numbers. His fingers twitched as if counting the years, maybe counting some unit of time longer than years. With a degree of certainty, he said, "Two million of yer Earth years."

"Are you telling me you are two million years old?" said the reporter, quite shocked at the answer.

"Correct. The Good Lord put me here back at a time when He had just started to bring humanity down out of the trees and onto the plains. Even the most primitive versions of man wished for things, ya know? They were simple wishes, though, wishes for food and shelter and protection from wild animals. That sort of thing. But because there were not many humans on Earth, and because their wishes were rather simplistic, it gave me time to develop my farm, organize my fields, and hone the receipt and delivery of wishes. Oh, and let me add one more thought. I think the Good Lord conceived of the wish as a means for the creatures He had created to communicate with Him. They do live in different dimensions, after all."

The reporter took off his sun-faded fedora and ran his fingers through his hair. "Okay. Makes sense. Though I must admit to still having a hard time believing you are as old as you claim to be." He went on. "During my last visit, you listed the names of the fellows who deliver the 'wish seeds' and take away the fully grown wishes. Gabriel, Raphael, Jophiel, and Cameal. It occurred to me after I got home these are the names of archangels. Are you telling me there really are archangels?"

"Of course, there are archangels. Seven of them. Three of them, though, aren't much involved with the whole business of wish management. Uriel, Michael, and

Zadkiel are all off doing other business. I'm just not quite sure what that is, though."

"Wow. I never thought I would be tripping over archangels when I accepted this writing assignment! Then am I to assume there are also angels in this realm or perhaps some other realm of which you might be aware?"

"Most certainly. In fact, my earlier comment, that I manage this whole operation by myself, was not entirely correct. Angels do help me determine when wishes are ready to be harvested. And they help me to know which wishes might require review and approval by the Good Lord Himself."

"Really?" said the reporter shifting his gaze from the farmer out to the fields. "So how exactly does that work? If a wish is ready for harvest, do they pick it?"

"No. Their contributions are a bit more subtle. They usually work while I'm asleep. So, I don't see them do what it is they do. But when I go out in the morning to inspect the fields, I will often come across a white ribbon tied to a branch with a wish ready to be harvested. I'll collect the wish and take it back with me to the barn, crate it up with all of the other recently harvested wishes, and send it off with the afternoon pickup."

"This is getting more and more interesting. You do know the folks on Earth don't have the slightest clue about any of this. In fact, I'm starting to get a bit concerned maybe such knowledge might be abused in some manner. Think about it. My article could start a worldwide frenzy of wishing. You could get more wishes than you can handle."

"Hmmm. Yep. I suppose yer right."

"So why would you agree to meet with me, allow me to publish a story about you, this place, and what it is you do here?"

"I dunno. I never really thought about it much. I might have to have a chat with Gabriel about this. Yep, I just might."

The farmer continued to stare out at the fields while the reporter scribbled some thoughts in his notebook.

"Before I go, I have one more question for you. Is that okay?"

"Sure. Fire away."

"All right. Tell me. Have you ever made any wishes of your own? I mean, you have been here tending everyone's wishes for an untold number of years, all alone. Have you ever wished for a companion? Someone with whom you can share your life?"

"Ya ask a lot of interesting questions," replied the farmer.

"That's my job," said the reporter.

"For right now, lemme just say I have all I need. I just don't find myself wanting much of anything. As for being alone? No. It doesn't bother me. Nope. Not one bit."

"I want to thank you again for your willingness to answer my questions and to share your story with me. I do appreciate it. Any chance on my next visit, I could accompany you when you go out into the fields to inspect the wishes?"

"Oh, sure. It would be my pleasure."

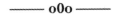

The reporter, never sure about how the passage of time differed from one dimensional plane to another dimensional plane, sent word to the farmer letting him know about plans for his next visit. He wasn't certain how the farmer received the messages, but he did seem to get them and was ready to receive the reporter.

Upon his arrival this time, the reporter found the farmer waiting for him at the site where the dimensional portal always seemed to materialize. A quick look up at the sky and the position of the sun allowed him to make an educated guess about the time of day. Redirecting his gaze at the farmer, he said, "Good morning. Thanks so much for meeting me. Am I to assume we are going for a walk in the fields?"

The farmer flashed his usual smile and nodded his head up and down. "Absolutely. Thought ya might like to see things up close and personal." The farmer extended his right arm and pointed to one of the fields up the road just a bit.

As they walked through the field, looking at all of the wishes hanging from their branches, they came upon a wish shriveled up and black, just barely clinging onto its branch. The farmer reached over, carefully finding the stem of the wish, then giving it a gentle tug. The dead wish let go of its grip.

"What makes a wish die?" asked the reporter.

"Could be for any number of reasons," answered the farmer. "In this case, the wisher has died, died before his or her wish could grow and be delivered. Too bad. But there are other possibilities. Take, for example, when two individuals wish for opposite outcomes. One person wants a thing to happen. The other person doesn't want a thing to happen. There can be only one outcome, ya know? And so, one wish will die."

"Sure. I can see it."

"Another example might be the Good Lord doesn't want a wish to be granted. He is the Big Boss of everything, ya know?"

The two men continued walking between the rows of plants, heading farther and farther away from the road. Subtle rises and dips filled the terrain. The countryside was very picturesque, something like one might see in a travel magazine or in photographs of the vineyards on Italian hillsides.

As they walked along, the reporter asked, "I'm to assume you have some sort of ability to read these wishes, to know something about the wisher, perhaps even know why it was they wished the wish they did?"

"Yep, a good assumption," said the farmer as he reached for one very large, but not yet ripe, wish. "Take this wish here, for example. It is from a parent wrongfully accused of some very terrible things. She lost custody of her children. The fruit is so large because it has been growing here for quite some time. I can only guess the wish is not ripe yet because the Good Lord has yet to approve the wish."

"Wow," sighed the reporter. "How about this wish over here? It seems very small but appears to be almost ripe."

The farmer laughed. "Oh, that one's easy. It is from a little boy who is wishing for a particular toy train. The wish is scheduled to be picked tomorrow. I believe it is a birthday present. I expect I'll see a white ribbon on its branch tomorrow mornin'."

"So, it is obvious some wishes are small and simple, and some wishes are serious and perhaps not so easy to grant."

"That's right," agreed the farmer.

"I can't help thinking about the wish back there, the one about the parent separated from her children. A serious situation, to be sure. I wonder if the parent might be better off sending a prayer directly to the Good Lord rather than sending a wish to you," proposed the reporter.

The sun, now at its highest point in the sky, caused the reporter to stop for a moment to wipe the sweat from his brow. The farmer waited patiently.

"It just occurred to me," said the reporter as they started walking again. "What is the difference between a wish and a prayer, anyway? Seems like there might be some overlap."

"Good question," replied the farmer. "The simple answer is this. Prayers . . . wishes . . . they all come through this place. But to answer yer question, wishes tend to be things granted by other people whereas prayers require the Good Lord's review and approval before they can be granted."

"Okay. I see. So, what happens if you receive a wish from someone which should have been a prayer?"

"Believe it or not, it happens quite frequently," the farmer commented.

"So, what do you do, then?"

"Well, after the wishes are delivered every morning, I do go through them and make certain each wish is really a wish and not a prayer. If I find something that's a prayer, I set it aside for special treatment. When Raphael arrives for the afternoon pickup, I let him know a prayer has come in. He'll deliver it to the Big Boss for review and approval. If approval is granted, I can plant it. Treat it just like any other wish."

"So, is there some other dimensional plane where prayers are reviewed and approved?" queried the reporter.

"A nice piece of deductive reasoning, my reporter friend. Truth is, I don't know what happens beyond the confines of this place. Perhaps one of yer fellow inhabitants of Earth might one day come across another dimensional plane, and you might get an answer to your question. But for now, I think it's time we head back to the road, and I'll let ya get back home."

The reporter returned to the farmer's dimension the next day. After resuming the seats they occupied on his previous visits, the reporter asked about the passage of time and how it seems to differ from dimension to dimension.

"So," the reporter started off, "according to my calendar, it was yesterday when I last visited you, when we walked through the fields. What about according to your calendar? When was my last visit?"

The farmer initiated his usual habit of rocking back and forth as he mulled over the question. "Hmmm. I don't really know. Might have been yesterday, or the day before yesterday, or maybe last week. Maybe longer, maybe shorter. Just really hard to know."

"Really?" queried the reporter. "I don't understand how it is you wouldn't know."

The farmer stared out at the fields of wish trees. "See, here's the thing. When yer as old as I am, and when yer not particularly concerned with the passage of time, or with yer own mortality, time doesn't become such an important commodity."

The reporter couldn't think of an immediate response.

"Now for yer fellow inhabitants of planet Earth, yer all mortal. Ya have birth and death. Ya live finite lives. That's how it's always been and, I suppose, that's how it will always be. Unless, of course, the Good Lord steps in to change things."

"Yes. I see your point," replied the reporter. "But speaking of birth and death, you raise another issue. As I was reviewing my notes from my previous visits, it seems to me you have quite a bit of knowledge about how things work in the greater, grander Universe. Might you be able to shed some light on questions us mere mortals have pondered throughout the ages?"

"Maybe. Maybe not. I am not omnipotent, ya know?"

"Okay. But I would regret it if I didn't at least try. Let's start at the beginning, the beginning of everything. If you can answer, how did the universe begin?"

A broad smile came across the farmer's face. He started to move his head slowly from side to side. After a minute or two, he said, "Let me answer yer question with another question. Can a human being witness their own birth in real-time?"

"No, of course not! Ah, okay. I think I see where you're going with this. The universe, or anything in it, cannot know how it came into being because it can't witness its own beginning."

"Ya understand. Good."

The reporter opened up his backpack and retrieved his notebook. Turning to the page with questions for the farmer he had scribbled the previous evening. His memory refreshed, he looked up and said, "On an earlier visit, I asked you if you had ever wished for something for yourself. I suggested you might have wished for a companion. You said 'no.' But I can't help but wonder, do you ever get lonely?"

"Lonely?" The farmer gave a silent laugh. "What do ya mean? I have visits every morning from the fellows who deliver the wishes and return every evening to collect the newly harvested wishes."

"Yes, yes. I know," agreed the reporter. "But what about at night when you're alone in your farmhouse, by yourself. Do you ever wish you had someone with whom to share time? Are you not lonely then?"

"Ya know, I've never really thought about it to tell ya the truth." A gust of wind blew in from the western fields, causing some of his hair to fall into his face. He brought up his hand and pushed the fallen hair back behind his ear. "Why do ya ask?"

"It just seems like after centuries of living life as you do, you might make a wish for yourself, for someone to talk to late at night, for someone to spend time with."

"If I were a betting man, which I'm not, I might guess yer the one who is lonely," he said pointing his finger at the reporter, then sitting back to continue his rocking, a sort of self-satisfied grin on his face.

"Guilty as charged," admitted the reporter. "Ever since I was a young man, I thought about how great it would be if I had a partner, a girlfriend, a mate. I often look around at my friends and coworkers and they all seem to be married or involved in some sort of committed relationship. Then I think to myself, how does one go about finding someone appropriate, or acceptable, or suitable?"

The farmer stopped rocking. "Even though I've been around for a couple of million years, I've never had a special someone, so I'm no expert on relationships. I can't help ya there. Ever thought about making a wish? Ever thought about offering up a prayer?"

"I can't say I have, though I might have without really meaning to. Who knows? But since I've met you, seen your dimension, and learned about how wishes work, I just might think about it."

"All right," said the farmer. "Just remember what I told ya about the difference between wishes and prayers. A wish might be easier to grant if it's directed toward a certain person, a certain potential partner. The wish might go something like, 'I wish so-and-so . . . whatever the person's name is . . . might become interested in having a relationship with me.' A prayer would have to be reviewed and approved by the Good Lord and might go something like this, 'Dear God, please find me a suitable partner.'"

"Understood. Thank you," said the reporter. "I'll give the matter some thought when I get home. I'll just add one more thing. The older I get, the more set in my ways I become. I'm concerned I might not be as willing to compromise on issues as I once was. Relationships seem to involve a lot of compromise."

"Now that I can't help ya with!" The farmer laughed.

"Okay, then. Best I head home, I suppose. Thanks for your time. And thanks for your suggestions. Much appreciated."

The reporter got up to make his way down the stairs and head up the road to activate the inter-dimensional portal.

TWO

JONATHAN ARGENT RELISHED THE freedom his position as a senior investigative reporter brought. It meant he didn't always have to get up every morning, fight rush hour traffic, and deal with office politics. He could come and go as he pleased. And with each successive award he received for his work, he was granted more and more independence. But at times, his boss wanted him in the office, to suggest a new story idea, to check on the progress of his assignments, or to rearrange his priorities. And today was one of those days.

The reporter woke up early, got dressed, made himself some breakfast, and left his apartment hoping to beat at least some of the traffic and find a good parking place, one close to the office building. After getting settled in his office and organizing his notes, he headed down the hall to the corner suite of the executive editor.

With telephones on each side of his head, the editor barked out orders to staff members throughout the organization. He motioned Argent to enter and take a seat. The reporter did so and waited patiently, as he usually did when the editor called for him. Once the telephones were placed back in their cradles, pleasantries were exchanged.

175

"So. Tell me. How goes the dimension-hopping?"

"Hmmm. Not certain where to start. First of all, the concept of alternate dimensions coexisting with our own is mind-blowing enough. But when you contemplate there is now the means to travel between those dimensions, it's totally amazing. And then there is what one finds when one arrives in the alternate dimension. Things are . . . different."

"How so?" asked the editor while silencing a ringing phone.

"Well, things which have no physical attributes here in our dimension possess form and substance in another dimension."

"You mean like wishes? I've read your status report. If I didn't know better, I might think it is pure fantasy and you're sitting at home writing science fiction, not out doing investigative reporting."

"Sure. But I am out there. And I'm doing my darnedest to come up with a way to document my experiences, knowing full well most folks are going to think the whole thing is one-hundred-percent pure gobbledygook."

"Jonathan, you are a terrific writer. You have a whole wall full of awards. I'm sure you'll come up with something. I just don't want your article about this Wishbringer fellow to read like a book report. What your article needs is some pizzazz, something sensational!"

The reporter looked down at the floor, contemplating his boss's comment, wondering how to respond, then offered, "With all due respect, sir. I think the farming of wishes in an alternate dimension is sensational enough. This is a respectable news organization after all, not a tabloid looking to saturate the public with the latest wacko theory. So, I'm not sure 'pizzazz' is appropriate."

"No. You're right," agreed the editor. "But folks aren't going to take your assertions of an alternate dimension with fields of wish plants and archangels who act as delivery boys for the farmer seriously. You don't have any real proof."

"I know. I have thought of that. It's been suggested I should make a wish for myself, maybe a series of wishes, a little one for something simple, one for something a bit more substantial, and one big wish . . . perhaps for something not so easily granted."

"And you believe all of this, do you?"

"Well, if you saw the fields of plants with their branches full of wishes, and saw the care with which this farmer fellow treats his calling? Yes, I am convinced. But I understand your skepticism."

"Okay. So, what if I was to make a wish? Say, for something relatively unobtrusive? Let's say, I wish for a sandwich, ham and cheese on rye, slightly toasted. And I wish for it to appear on my desk right now?"

The editor looked down at his paper-filled desktop, waited for a few seconds, then said, "See what I mean? Nothing. How are people expected to take any of this seriously? Your reputation will suffer. But more importantly, the reputation of this organization will suffer if this story isn't delivered just right."

"I get it. But let me just say the absence of a sandwich materializing on your desk doesn't diminish my experiences and what is going on out in the greater universe."

"I believe you. But there will be those who won't. You're going to have to sell it to our readers, convince them."

"Okay, sir. Lemme see what I can do," said the reporter as he scrawled a few comments in his notebook.

"Great. Check-in with me in a week or so. This could be the biggest story of the year . . . of the decade . . . heck, maybe even ever. I want it done right. I have faith in you, Argent. Don't let me down."

The reporter got up, gave a subtle nod to the editor, and left.

Jonathan Argent returned home that evening. After unlocking the door and walking in, he set his things down in their usual spots on his dining room table. The apartment was quiet and lifeless. He had crossed space and time to visit another dimension, an adventure millions of individuals only dreamed of making, and yet here he was again. Alone. In his small and quite plainly decorated apartment. The place could definitely stand a woman's touch. But where in the world, how in the world, was he ever going to find someone who would want to share life with him?

And then there were the words of his editor, saying the story about the farmer needed some pizzazz. And what did he call the farmer? The Wishbringer? That's right. Good name. It's a keeper. Anyway, the editor wants the story to be sensational. But the process of making wishes and getting them granted was not some joy ride, something with which to be trifled. The reporter had never intended to make this story "sensational."

He walked over to the picture window, opened the blinds, and stood there for a long moment, looking out over the city. All of those people out there, all making wishes, sending them out to a dimension they don't even know exists. Sending them out to someone who will plant them, tend to them, read them, perhaps even judge them.

He sat down in his favorite chair. The words the farmer said about being alone came to mind. The farmer did have a habit of answering questions with questions. "Why do ya ask?" he had said. Why, indeed.

The reporter knew the answer to the question well enough. He was the one alone, and his apartment mirrored that fact. It was empty and quiet and without color.

So, what if he did make a wish for someone special? A soulmate? Someone who might add a little something extra to his life. It would be the perfect way to see if this whole wish thing really worked. Now, all he had to do was figure out how to make his wish known to the farmer, to the Wishbringer.

But the farmer had also said wishes could only be granted by other people. The reporter recounted the farmer's suggestion to name a specific individual and wish they might suddenly become interested in him. The difficulty with this approach was simply he didn't know many single women, especially women who might be just the right amount of this and have just right amount of that, someone who might meet his rather stringent criteria of acceptability. *A problem requiring additional thought*, he concluded.

He got up, went to the kitchen, started boiling water for rice, and cutting up vegetables for stir-fry. A question came to mind. How long might it take for the farmer to receive the wish? Still not knowing how time passed in the farmer's dimension, perhaps a few days? A week? A month? Yes, another visit would need to be made. Guidance from the farmer would need to be sought.

The reporter felt pleased with the plan, more pleased than he had felt about anything in a long time.

Then he realized he never asked the farmer how one goes about making a wish official. Does one have to write a letter and mail it to himself? No, that can't be it. Not if a little boy wishing for a toy train gets his wish. He would need to ask that question, as well.

Several days went by before the reporter could get a message off to the farmer, requesting some time with him to discuss the issue of wishing for a prospective partner and the mechanics of making such a wish. By now, his trips to the farmer's dimension had become almost routine. When he arrived, the reporter found the farmer sitting in his usual rocking chair on the porch, waiting for him with a pleasant smile and a friendly greeting.

The reporter settled himself in the other rocker, took a moment to compose himself, and started describing his thoughts about finding someone with whom he could share his life.

"So, I have given a great deal of thought to my loneliness and to the possibility of wishing for someone special. I was wondering if you might help me?"

"Okay. What did you have in mind?"

"Well, my first problem is this. There isn't anyone, and for the record, it would be a female anyone, anyone who is single in my sphere of acquaintances. Almost all of the women I know are either married or already in a committed relationship."

"Hmmm. Yes. That would make it difficult to direct a wish at a specific individual."

"So, what would happen if I left the specifics up to

you, or the wish trees, or the Good Lord, or whoever it might be, that would set the wheels in motion, so to speak?"

"That could work. But there would be a lot of open variables. Ya might not end up with an exact match," warned the farmer.

"Yep. I think I see where you are going. I do understand the natural course of things would have me meeting someone, learning their life, and then, if things were working out, moving into a more serious relationship."

"That's right," acknowledged the farmer.

"I just don't know how to go about this or what to wish for."

"Well, like ya said earlier, ya could leave it up to fate. Might just work out for ya. But ya know," continued the farmer, "wishes are funny things. Lots of wishes arrive here without the wisher giving his or her wish much forethought, without considering the consequences of their wish should it come true. It's sort of like asking a carpenter to build a house, but not giving him a complete set of plans."

"Understood. So, my next question is, how does one make a wish official? How does a wish find its way to you and get processed?"

"That's the easy part. Ya simply speak it out loud," said the farmer in a very confident voice.

"Really? I don't need to write a letter and send it to . . . oh, I don't know . . . myself?"

"Nope. The universe will hear ya. There are lots of angels on Earth, lots and lots of them. And they listen for everyone's wishes and prayers. When they hear someone utter a wish or say a prayer, they send it on up to Gabriel or whoever is on duty, and the wish or prayer is crated up and scheduled for delivery to me."

"Wow. You make this whole thing seem like it is some sort of factory. Raw materials go in one end of the plant, down an assembly line, and the finished product comes rolling out the other end."

"I know it might be difficult for ya to grasp how things work when it comes to wishes, but that is the reality of things," confirmed the farmer.

"Huh," the reporter muttered, still not entirely convinced. "One last question for you today, then. How long do you think it might take for a wish I make to be processed, a wish for an appropriate partner to come into my life? I'm curious. On my first visit, you said some wishes grow rather quickly, some take years to develop, some never grow at all. I guess I'm also curious because if this all works out, I might want to include this experience in the article I'm writing."

The farmer sat rocking away for a bit before answering. "See, here's the thing. Every wish is different, different because of the wisher, the level of certainty with which the wish is made, the appropriateness of the wish, and the degree of complexity in arranging things in yer world such that the wish might come to fruition. It's just really, really hard to give ya a hard and fast estimate."

"Understood."

"Now in yer case, I've had the pleasure of meeting ya, of getting a feel for what sort of a person ya are, and for discussing some of the particulars of yer wish. It might be I can give yer wish some amount of special handling. But there are other issues over which I have no control, things like the effect of the soil, how often the celestial rains come during the growth of yer wish. So, ya see, I can't make any promises."

"This all helps. I think I need to return home, do some thinking, and when I'm ready, I'll make my wish.

I'll be able to do it with a certain amount of confidence, knowing you're here working your magic."

"Fair enough," the farmer said as he got up to shake the reporter's hand.

"Thanks again for everything," offered the reporter. "Until next time?"

With that, the reporter left the farmer rocking away on his porch.

THREE

THE REPORTER RETURNED TO HIS dimension on planet Earth, spending the next several weeks thinking about his wish. He very much wanted to be specific about the type of woman he would like. *After all, if this works out,* he thought, *I would be spending the rest of my life with this person.* But the more he contemplated a potential wish, the more he realized how many variables needed to be considered when defining the sort of person he wanted.

Every so often, he would trip over a parameter he couldn't seem to assess, couldn't analyze, couldn't come up with a decision about which he felt good. He soon realized too much of a specific attribute might lead to one problem, but too little might lead to another problem. And how does one rate each personality trait, anyway? It wasn't like things such as a sense of humor or a sense of adventure or self-confidence have scales allowing one to arrive at a specific setting, he might be able to include in his wish. At times the reporter started to feel like he was in a wish store, standing at the counter, ordering up a person, telling the angel behind the counter to hold the mayo and double the ketchup. Is this really how he wanted to find a soulmate?

The reporter eventually set all of his thinking aside, deciding he needed to let the whole project simmer for a bit. Perhaps some time away from the subject matter would help. So, he focused on completing his article about the Wishbringer, leaving out any mention of his attempt to wish for a special someone.

A few more weeks slipped by. From time to time, the reporter would have a thought or two about what characteristics he might want in a potential mate. He started a list. And as the list grew, he began organizing the various characteristics into categories. One category was for personality, one category for physical appearance, and another category was for likes and dislikes the person might have.

Sometimes he would sit down, read through the list, and conclude no such person could exist. And even if they did, the chances of his meeting up with this idyllic individual were quite likely next to nil.

Finally, after all of the soul-searching and pondering, he decided to make his wish. With his neatly organized list, he stood in the middle of his living room looking out his picture window, raised his arms as if praying for rain, and started to recite his wish.

"Dearest Wishbringer. I am now officially making my wish for a person who I believe will make a perfect mate for me, someone who has the following characteristics." The reporter read his list aloud, making sure he spoke slowly and clearly. After he finished reciting all the parameters, he continued. "And finally, Wishbringer, I wish this individual would be made obvious to me so I need not wonder whether it is this person or that person. I send this wish to you, for your special handling. May it come to fruition in a timely manner. Thank you so much for helping me in my quest. God bless you."

The reporter placed his list back on the dining room table so it might remind him of his wish. He had great faith the Wishbringer would receive the wish, and plant it in the field designated for wishes involving love. He knew the Wishbringer had not been able to estimate the amount of time it would take for the wish to grow. But the reporter didn't really care at this point. He felt so much better for having been through this exercise and for having made the wish.

More weeks went by. The reporter continued his life much as he had before he made his first inter-dimensional journey. He conducted investigations for various other assignments the editor gave him. He spent quiet evenings in his apartment writing. And he made his occasional commutes to the office. Everything seemed to be progressing without any major bumps in the road. He even filed away his wish list. One thing did occur to him from time to time. He had not experienced any feelings of loneliness since making his wish. For that, he was grateful.

FOUR

"GOOD MORNING, DEAR," said the reporter's wife.

The reporter heard the salutation through the mists of his early morning reverie. He rolled over without opening his eyes.

"Hey, sleepyhead, you're going to miss your appointment if you don't wake up."

The words, the voice, the shaking of his shoulder, all forced him out of his sleep, forced him to open his eyes. He immediately recoiled at the sight of a strange woman in his bedroom.

"Who are you?" The reporter blurted out without thinking. He knew he had not been out drinking the night before. He had not picked up anyone at the local bar. His brain struggled to wake up, to make sense of things. Then a single, barely believable, thought shot through his head.

My wish! It's been granted!

"I'm your wife, silly." There was a pause. "Are you all right? Are you feeling okay?"

The reporter pushed away from her, his thoughts flashing back to his discussion with the farmer, about the need to be specific with one's wish. Another thought struck the reporter like a bolt of lightning. *He had forgotten to include one key criterion in his wish for a companion, one significant omission when he said 'I wish this individual would be made obvious to me so I need not wonder whether it is this person or that person.'* Waking up next to someone who claimed to be your wife certainly met that part of the wish!

But he didn't know her name!

The reporter hemmed and hawed. He didn't know what to do or what to say. Finally, he said, "No. Actually, I don't feel very well. My head is spinning, and I feel nauseous. I think I need to take a shower. I'll stop in to see the doctor on my way to the office."

"Are you certain you're going to be okay? You look like you've just seen a ghost."

"Ummm, yes. Thanks for your concern. I better get up and get the show on the road."

The reporter took his shower, got dressed, skipped his usual breakfast, and left for work, leaving his wife without a kiss or an "I love you." As the door to his apartment closed behind him, he didn't see the perplexed look on his wife's face. His mind was racing in a million different directions. This was most certainly not how he had anticipated his wish would be granted. He needed some time to think.

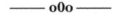

The reporter went straight to work. He felt terrible for lying to this woman about stopping to see the doctor. But he couldn't help that right now. He needed to calm down, needed to figure out how to respond to this completely unanticipated situation.

Out of habit, he checked his voice messages before starting any work. There was one message from the editor, asking him to check in about the Wishbringer Project, as he had come to call it.

He got up, walked down the hall, found the editor's door shut, and then gave several light knocks. The editor was likely on an important call, so the reporter stood in the hall waiting, curious to know if this was a simple check-in, or if the editor had some specific agenda in mind. Maybe it was taking too long to write the Wishbringer story. Maybe he had chosen the wrong approach. Maybe the editor wasn't happy with some aspect of the story. Or perhaps the article didn't have the punch the editor wanted. He realized his imagination was out of control. Not surprising, considering the events of earlier this morning.

The door finally opened, and the editor turned to head back to his desk without saying a word. As he sat down, the reporter saw the editor's tie was loose and his face was expressionless. The reporter closed the door behind him and settled himself in one of the two chairs facing the large oak desk.

The editor cleared his throat. "That was the Department of Inter-dimensional Exploration on the phone."

"Really? Should I ask what they wanted?"

"You're not going to be happy about this. After reading the draft version of your article I sent them, they've changed their minds regarding our investigation of this Wishbringer and his dimension. They're reversing their decision. They don't want us publishing your piece on your inter-dimensional jaunts."

The reporter sat in silence. His head slowly started turning from side to side.

"And there's more," continued the editor. "Effective immediately, you are banned from any more trips to the Wishbringer's dimension, or any other dimension, for that matter."

The editor allowed the reporter to absorb the news before delivering the final demand of the Department of Inter-dimensional Exploration.

"One last thing. They are requiring you hand over all records of your visits, whether they be hard copies or electronic files, any tape recordings of interviews or any other evidence proving the existence of alternate dimensions. And finally, you are forbidden to speak to anyone, ever, about what you have found or what it is you know about the Wishbringer and his dimension, or that we now possess the ability to visit other dimensions."

The reporter took a deep breath and slowly exhaled. He bit his lip and tried putting all of the pieces into place. Before he could say anything, the editor put his notes down, looked at the reporter, and said, "Don't take any of this the wrong way. What you wrote was excellent. Maybe this is a backhanded compliment, who knows? But you did suggest knowledge of this dimension, knowledge of what wishes are, and how they are processed might not be such a good thing for the average human to know. You might be doing humanity a huge favor."

The reporter sat stunned, only half-listening to the editor. His thoughts went immediately to the Wishbringer, not being able to extend a proper farewell, to thank him for his time, and for teaching him about what goes on out in the vastness of time and space. But what was weighing on his mind more than that was what to do about his new wife. Within the span of two hours, his life had been turned upside down. And now he wouldn't be able to talk to the farmer or seek his advice. Was he just supposed to wish his wife back into nonexistence? Could this even be done? He wondered if one could reverse a wish. He desperately wanted the help of the Wishbringer, desperately needed the help of the Wishbringer.

Finally, the reporter managed to say, "I understand. I can't say I'm okay with everything, but I do understand it. I most certainly would have been thrilled to have my name associated with one of the most revealing stories in human history. But I am grateful my name will not be linked to knowledge which might trigger absolute chaos. If events were to become uncontrollable, even deadly, I'm not sure I would want to carry any of the blame for that."

"You seem to be accepting this much better than I thought you would. But still," the editor stopped in mid-sentence. "You seem like there might be something else bothering you about all of this."

"And you would be right," sighed the reporter. He thought about what he should say, what words he might use to express what he was feeling. "There is an old adage. It goes something like this: be careful what you wish for, you just might get it. I wished for something, and I got it. And, in retrospect, I may have made a huge mistake."

The reporter's eyes drifted up toward the ceiling as he spoke. He couldn't look at the editor.

"Dare I ask what you wished for?"

"You said several weeks ago you wanted some pizzazz in the article, something making the story sensational. During one of my visits to the Wishbringer, I couldn't help but notice he lived alone, and apparently had done so for an amazingly long time. I asked him if he ever felt lonely, if he had ever wished for companionship. He answered he had never thought about it. But he quite astutely recognized loneliness was an issue I faced. And he was right."

"You feel lonely?"

"Sure. Look around at the staff. Almost everyone here is either married or is in a committed relationship. People are talking about things coupled people talk about. Their social lives, their vacations, their kids, those sorts of things. I can't bring anything to those conversations. All I have to talk about is my work, whatever story it is I'm currently writing. And so, in part to test this whole wish thing, to see if it might work for me and, in part, because I am lonely, I wished for a companion, a partner.

"During one of my visits to the Wishbringer, I raised this issue. We discussed the possibility of me registering a formal wish for someone special, a soulmate. He made it pretty clear to me I should be very specific about my wish. So, I went home, thought about it a great deal, and put together a list of specifics, things like beliefs, looks, likes, dislikes. After thinking I had covered all the bases, I made my wish."

"There's no harm in that, is there?" reassured the editor. "People wish for a special someone all the time. You didn't do anything anybody hasn't done. Give yourself a break."

"Perhaps. But I omitted one critical caveat when making my wish. You see, I wished this individual would be made obvious to me, so I need not wonder whether it was this person or that person."

"Okay. That would eliminate a lot of the guesswork from the whole dating thing," commented the editor. "It would save a lot of time, too."

The reporter took a deep breath. "This morning, I woke up next to a woman who claims to be my wife. I've never met this woman before. The worst part about it is, I don't even know her name."

The editor sat motionless, then uttered a single word. "Wow."

"Yep. My wish came true. Most relationships start out as casual acquaintances, then grow into friendships. And if things are right, and the two have enough shared likes and dislikes, enough in common, things develop into love and a committed relationship."

"Yep. That's generally how things go."

"But not in my case. I went to bed last night as a single person and woke up this morning with a strange woman next to me. And apparently, she has been my wife for some time. No gradual getting to know one another, no growing close over time, no chance to see if the other person is a good fit. And the worst part about all of this is, I'm not quite certain I know what to do about it. I had hoped to make one last trip to visit the farmer, the Wishbringer, to seek some guidance. But now, I can't."

"And this is all for real?"

"Oh, yes. I can introduce her to you if you'd like."

"No, I don't think it's necessary. I'll take your word for it."

"So, to bring this back around to your point about there being something else bothering me? Yes. I wanted to ask the Wishbringer if there might be something I can do to reverse the situation. Is there is such a thing as reversing a wish, or unwishing? And would that mean I would be wishing a person out of existence? Sort of feels like I'd be killing someone, committing murder. I'm not that kind of a person. But on the other hand, am I supposed to live with someone with whom I don't know for the rest of my life? It feels like punishment for making an ill-conceived wish."

The two men sat in silence for a few minutes. The sounds from the street filtered up from below. The occasional honk of a horn, the blowing of a policeman's whistle, a distant siren.

The editor took a long sip of his now cold coffee, set down his mug slowly and deliberately and thought, *maybe a shot of whiskey might be more appropriate.*

"Argent, you're a good man. Quite frankly, I've often wondered why some woman hasn't come along and claimed you for her own. But finding the right person isn't always as simple as going to the store and picking out the model you want. Sometimes it is simply the result of being at the right place at the right time. We can't know in advance when or where that might be. Seems to me you wanted to skip the fun part, going out on dates, learning another's life."

The reporter shifted his weight in the chair and forced himself to look at the editor. "I know," he said quietly.

"Look, you've been through a lot in the last few weeks. You've experienced things no one has ever experienced before. I know if I said take a week or two off, it probably wouldn't help much right now, especially if you don't want to go home and be with this woman. And you said she professes to be your wife?"

"Yep. Someone I theoretically had made to order just for me but forgot to include an ideal name for her. Sarah? Sally? Sophie? I don't know. I was having a tough time this morning before I left home. I felt so incredibly stupid for not having any clue what her name might be. I didn't think to look for it in the pile of mail sitting on the dining room table. After we're done here, I'm going to go back to my office and see if I can't find a copy of the marriage license online. Maybe I can at least learn her name before I have to go home."

"Okay, okay. I will give a call to the Department of Inter-dimensional Exploration, tell them something, though I'm not quite sure what yet, and see if they won't allow you one more trip to see this Wishbringer fellow. Give me a few hours."

"Fair enough."

"I'm not promising anything," warned the editor. "And, Argent, in the meantime, if everything you say is true and the Wishbringer put this woman together for you based on your criteria, then maybe you should give her a chance, you know? Don't be so quick to wish away the very thing for which you've wanted your whole life."

"Good advice and thanks. Until I get used to this whole thing, I'll probably be spending a bit more time in the office. And, oh yes, I'll start pulling together all of my notes and records for you. Wouldn't want the folks at the Department to think I'm being uncooperative."

"Good man. Now try to relax. Let's keep our collective fingers crossed. Okay? And remember, not a word about this dimension-hopping to anyone, especially your wife."

"Got it, sir."

The reporter stood up, the two men shook hands, and the reporter returned to his office.

The reporter sat down, turned on his computer, and looked up the address for the Clerk's Office at the County Circuit

Court. When he arrived at the correct web page, he entered his name. The next screen asked him a few questions. He typed in the requested information and in a few seconds, an electronic copy of a marriage license popped up on his screen, complete with his wife's name, their wedding date, and to his utter astonishment, his signature.

How in the world?

Returning his attention to his wife's name. Desirée DeCoeur. The reporter laughed to himself. *The universe is playing a little trick on me, no doubt. A loose translation of French words for 'desire of my heart.' Wonder if she goes by Dezzie? So, if I'm to remain with this woman for the rest of my life, I'll be forever reminded she is the embodiment of what I desired. Nice work, Universe.*

"And we've been married for two-and-a-half years," the reporter read out loud. He cocked his head to the side and thought, *if I've been married for over two years, how come my editor didn't know? And how is my signature on this document, and I have no memory of ever signing it? Something is very strange here. This is so not making sense.*

He printed off a copy of the marriage license and closed the web page. He sat in his office, staring at the wall, not knowing what to do. His first thought was to go home and explain everything to Desirée. But then he remembered the edict from the Department of Inter-dimensional Exploration.

What? I can't even tell my wife? Seriously? If I can't tell her the real story, that I wished her into existence, what other choice did I have? Play along? Do all of the learning about her I should have done while dating? She apparently knows me well enough.

Then he had another thought, one that made him laugh out loud. It was so outrageous. But it could work.

What if he told her he had been diagnosed with amnesia? Something straight out of soap opera scripts. Wouldn't the same set of circumstances be in effect? Require the same resolution?

The reporter set this option aside for the moment and made a feeble effort to get some work done, though he knew his productivity would take a hit today. Every time a thought or a possible solution came to mind, he would stop and write it down in his notebook. Maybe the editor might have some word back from the Department before the end of the day. Maybe, then, there might be a solution.

At three o'clock, the reporter's phone rang. The section's secretary asked him to come down to the editor's office. He hurried down the hall, wondering whether he should share any of his thoughts about the marriage license, about how long he had been married, and about using amnesia as a means to navigate this situation.

"Come on in," said the editor. "And shut the door behind you, please."

The reporter closed the door and reclaimed his usual seat. "Am I to assume you've had a conversation with a certain Department?"

"Correct." The editor leaned back in his chair and proceeded to roll up his sleeves. "It seems as though you've made quite an impression on the folks in their office."

"Really? A good impression, I'm assuming?"

"Oh, yes. And I'm not surprised. They appreciated your thoughts about the dangers of the population becoming aware of, not only the whole wish thing, but of humankind's newfound ability to journey to alternate dimensions. And I have to say they appreciated your willingness to forgo publication and meet all of their conditions."

"Not really much of a choice."

"Well, that being said, they have agreed to grant you one last trip to visit the farmer. Given there's an indefinable time difference between the dimensions, they didn't put any limit on the length of your visit."

"Got it."

"But they did have one stipulation. There is to be no wishing involved. So, I guess that means you don't have to worry about 'unwishing' your wife into oblivion."

"Agreed. And thank you, sir. I don't know what you told them, but I appreciate this. And if you speak with the Department again, please do pass on my gratitude."

"Lemme know how it goes, will you?"

"Sure thing. Now all I have to decide is when I will go. Probably in the next day or three. I have thought a great deal about your recommendation, though, that I should give this woman a chance. In theory, she was made to order."

"I think that's fair. Good luck, Argent."

FIVE

THE REPORTER OPENED THE DOOR to his apartment slowly, not quite sure what to expect. It occurred to him he didn't even know if his wife worked, stayed home, whether she had relatives nearby. Nothing. The feelings of guilt for being responsible for this situation welled up inside him, made him sick to his stomach. He was ashamed, embarrassed, and felt so stupid.

"What did the doctor say?" A voice came from the living room, followed by the sounds of her getting up from the sofa and walking across the hardwood floor toward him. He stood quietly, waiting for her. He wanted another look at her. He had rushed out this morning, wanting to get away. He had only a brief glance at her and her shoulder-length brown hair. That much he remembered.

As she came around the corner into the foyer, he gathered up his courage and softly said, "Amnesia. Well, partial amnesia."

"What? What in the world caused that?"

"The doctor said my short-term memory has somehow been compromised. My long-term memory is pretty much intact. Not sure how it happened."

She looked down at the floor, then managed, "And when you say your short-term memory has 'been compromised,' just exactly how far back is 'short term'?"

"Maybe three or four years. We're not certain yet." The reporter felt even worse for embellishing this lie he had concocted.

She looked up at him and began to reach out, then stopped short. "Dare I ask? Do you remember me?" He saw tears starting to roll down her cheeks. Perhaps she thought better of pushing herself onto him before she had learned the extent of his memory loss.

"I'm so very sorry. This must be so very painful for you. The truth is, I only remember little bits and pieces. I remember your name. I know we were married on September 10, coming up on three years ago." Another embellishment, more guilt and more shame.

"So this morning, when you woke up, did you know where you were?"

The reporter held out his hand to her. "Come on. Let's go into the living room and sit down while we talk." She took his hand, seemingly grateful he had not outright rejected her because of his memory loss.

She sat back down on the sofa, presumably where she had been sitting before he arrived home. He took his usual seat in his recliner. He looked at her and thought, *she is kind of cute. Plain, but definitely cute. Brown hair, brown eyes, just like I wished. Maybe this might work. Yes, maybe.*

"I've been so worried about you all day. I tried to call you once, at the office. But I didn't leave a message."

"I spent quite a bit of time down in the editor's office today. We're trying to tie up some loose ends on an article. It most certainly didn't help I couldn't remember much about my recent assignments. I think he was pretty concerned about things."

"So, what about the farmer, the Wishbringer? That assignment?" she asked.

The reporter felt a burst of adrenaline shoot through his entire body. His face must have appeared flushed.

"Are you okay? You look like you have a fever. Your face . . . it's red."

"I'll be all right in a minute. I've had a few spells like that today. The doctor said they would diminish as I slowly acclimate to my condition." More lying. The reporter hated what he was doing.

"Okay. But any time you want to go and lie down, just let me know."

"Agreed. You asked about the Wishbringer Project. That was the one thing about which the editor was most concerned. Unfortunately, I have almost no memory of anything having to do with that assignment." Another fabrication.

His wife thought for a moment, then proposed a theory. "You don't suppose your condition has anything to do with the Wishbringer, do you? I mean, what if he didn't want you writing about him or his dimension, about the wish trees. That just might make some sense, you know? If you can't remember anything about it, then you can't write about it, and the world won't learn the truth about wishes."

"Certainly plausible," agreed the reporter, mulling over the idea. "Actually, that seems very plausible." The reporter thought this theory was a nice touch to his lie. He was grateful his wife had come up with it.

"How about I fix you a drink? The usual?"

The reporter couldn't resist adding one more touch to his charade. "I hate to ask, but what is my usual?"

"A tequila sunrise with a dash of Cholula."

"Oh, right. Thank you for the reminder. Something tells me we will have to do this sort of thing for a while . . . at least until I can get my feet back on the ground."

"I understand. I am here for you, dear. We will get through this together."

As his wife headed off for the kitchen, the reporter thought to himself, *oh, my God. What have I done?*

The next morning the reporter did not recoil when his wife gently nudged him awake, asking him if he would like her to cook some breakfast. He opened his eyes slowly, wondering whether his wife would still be there, or whether the whole thing had been a dream or some sort of sick joke the universe was playing on him.

Convinced his wife was, in fact, still there and apparently quite real, he accepted the invitation. He made his way out to the dining room table, sat down, and took a sip from the glass of orange juice his wife had placed there for him.

"I'm so relieved you're at least a little bit back in the real world, that you didn't freak out when waking up this morning. How are you feeling today?" There was obvious concern in her voice.

"Well, physically, I'm feeling okay. My head is still a bit fuzzy, though. But as for my thoughts, things are still pretty jumbled up. Just when I think something might be making sense and I reach out to grab it and analyze it, it slips away. There is so much I can't pull together just yet. Thanks for asking."

"Of course! I'm worried about you."

The reporter watched as she flitted about the kitchen in her bathrobe and slippers, brewing coffee, making toast, and scrambling eggs. He wondered if this lie about having amnesia and this desire to undo everything he had done were mistakes. In this play-acting, he was feigning confusion about the last three years' events. But on the inside, there was most definitely confusion, confusion about the relationship he had longed for, the relationship now right here in front of him, but one about which he had no sense of certainty.

When everything was ready, she brought out mugs of steaming hot coffee and plates with the toast, eggs, and several pieces of strawberries all beautifully arranged.

"Wow. I do seem to recall your ability to serve up a nice breakfast." Another lie.

As they enjoyed their breakfast, his wife asked, "What do you plan to do today? Will you be working at home or going into the office?"

The reporter took a sip of his coffee and replied, "I need to head into work. The editor is concerned about some of the smaller assignments on which I've been working. He wants to debrief me, wants to make certain he knows where things are. I think he wants to assign some of these projects to other reporters. That's totally fine with me. I really want to take some time away from work, to try and get my head together. I should be home late this afternoon." One more deception to add to the growing list.

"Are you sure you are okay to drive?"

"Oh, yes. Remember, it is the short-term memory, not the long-term stuff. Thanks so much for a wonderful breakfast. And thank you for your concern and patience." The reporter carried his plate and mug out to the kitchen sink, leaving his wife sipping her coffee and staring out the picture window.

SIX

THE INTER-DIMENSIONAL PORTAL powered up. The technician gave him the go-ahead. The reporter stepped through the portal for what he knew would be his last trip to visit the farmer. Over these last weeks and months, he had grown rather fond of the farmer, his laid-back approach to life, and sense of peace and contentment.

When he arrived at the front porch of the farmer's home, he told the farmer everything that had happened since his last visit. He told the farmer about the woman appearing yesterday morning, his response, the fake amnesia, and all of the lies he told this new wife to avoid telling her the truth, the truth of which he had been ordered not to speak.

In his usual manner, the farmer sat and rocked, and pondered recent events before offering up any commentary.

"Ya do realize what is going on here? What's left in the crucible after everything else is burned away?"

"I'm not certain I know what you're getting at," said the reporter.

"If I recall yer wish," began the farmer, "it sounded as though ya wanted to avoid all the guesswork about what a potential partner might think of ya while dating, avoid the starts and stops, the incorrect assumptions, perhaps the occasional squabble, the pain brought about by being uncertain if a potential mate might still love ya. Am I correct?"

"You pegged it," admitted the reporter.

"And now, aren't ya going through a different set of challenging circumstances and uncertainties, things of yer own making? Ya see, Jonathan, ya can't escape such things, such conflicts, in life. Ya can only trade one conflict for another, trade one problem for another. Yer now paying the price for yer wish, and now I get the sense ya want me to solve yer problem for ya by undoing yer wish. And where will it end, my friend?"

The reporter sat without moving, without rocking. The weight of what the farmer had said made his heart ache.

The farmer sighed. "Here's the truth of it, Jonathan. I don't know if I can undo the wish or not. This will require review and approval from the Big Boss. The only thing I can offer ya with any degree of certainty is this: ya can stay here."

The reporter looked at the farmer in disbelief. "What?"

"Ya can stay here. But if ya decide to stay here, ya would have to help me tend the wish trees. I would actually welcome the help. I even have an extra bedroom upstairs ya could have. But this would be yer existence for a very, very long time. Millions of years, perhaps. For as long as humankind is present in the universe. Not certain I would call it immortality, but the point is, a decision to stay here would be irreversible. There would be no going back to Earth. Not ever. No second chance."

The reporter sat in silence. He thought about going

back and the work that would have to be done to create a life with Desirée. Part of him wanted very much to stay here, to undo his wish, to never again to think about the decisions required of him in any search for a partner, about guessing whether someone might be receptive to his advances, about fearing rejection, about the eventual loss of the loved one from one's life years down the road.

At last, the reporter asked, "If I decide to stay here, to live on this beautiful farm, what would I need to do?"

"Just do whatcha did when ya wished for yer wife. State yer wish out loud. An angel will hear it, it will be received here, and I will personally see to it ya find yer way here. Ya wouldn't need to worry about the inter-dimensional portal. But should ya decide to stay on Earth, with or without the company of Desirée, I'm giving ya one last wish."

"But the Department of Inter-dimensional Exploration gave me explicit orders not to make any more wishes," said the reporter in a concerned voice.

"I know. But consider this last wish a personal gift from me, for yer sacrifice, for giving up what would certainly be one of the greatest revelations in human history and letting go of the awards and fame it would have brought ya. Ya have given up an awful lot for the benefit of society. Ya've shown yerself to be quite wise. And I have it on good authority the Big Boss, the Good Lord, is also pleased with yer actions. Should ya choose to use this last wish, I will see to it the Department is not made aware of it. Ya won't suffer any harm or repercussions."

"I know I've said this many times before but thank you. Thank you so very much. I have learned some powerful and painful lessons in all of this. And I might just have one more to learn."

For a final time, Jonathan Argent got up from his rocking chair and shook hands with the farmer, the Wishbringer. He slowly walked down the stairs, out across the courtyard, and up the road. The shimmer of the inter-dimensional portal began to appear. The reporter turned around and gave one last wave before stepping into the light.

SEVEN

IT WAS LATE, ALMOST MIDNIGHT. Jonathan Argent sat in his office at home, thinking about all of the things that had happened over the last several weeks and months. He thought about the Wishbringer, his fields of mysterious plants, cultivating the wishes of the billions of people on planet Earth, and the choices he had made since his first visit to the farmer's dimension.

But mostly, he thought about what might happen if the inhabitants of Earth were made aware of how wishes were collected by angels, delivered to the Wishbringer, how they were planted, and how they were harvested. He wondered what the world would be like if people were to know the truth about wishes, that they were real things.

No. The world would become a very chaotic place if knowledge of dimensional travel were to become public and if the dimensional plane dedicated to the management of wishes were exploited.

Jonathan Argent made his decision. He would use his one last wish. And that wish would simply be this: he wished he had never made the inter-dimensional jumps, never met the Wishbringer, written his grand exposé, and never wished for a companion.

The reporter recalled the Wishbringer had said all one needed to do to make a wish official was utter it aloud. And so, the reporter spoke his wish, stating it loudly and carefully so there could be no misunderstanding it.

After he had done so, he knew in a dimensional plane far from planet Earth, a solitary farmer would receive a crate with his wish, perhaps casting a subtle glow, and that the wish would be planted in an appropriate field.

And for good measure, he uttered a prayer to the Good Lord that he would wake up one day and have no recollection of any of this.

The reporter crawled into bed next to his sleeping wife, closed his eyes, and quietly whispered, "I wish I had never wished."

——— oOo ———

The next morning the reporter woke up just as he always did, got ready for work just as he did on most days, and went to the office. He started his research on a newly assigned hush-hush government project. There was no wife or any memory of there ever having been a wife.

No sooner had he walked into his office then the telephone rang. The editor asked him to come down to his office to meet a new colleague.

"Good morning, Argent," said the editor in a rather exuberant voice. "I want to introduce ya to Desirée DeCoeur. She'll be working with ya on your new assignment. I'd appreciate it if ya would show her the ropes."

"It's a pleasure, Desirée." The reporter smiled and reached out to shake her hand.

"Please, call me Dezzie," she said, then added, "say . . . have we met before?"

—— oOo ——

"If you remain in me and my words remain in you, ask whatever you wish, and it will be done for you."
—JOHN 15:7

THE LAST SUNDAY OF SUMMER

(The Faithful and their Forfeit)

. . . .

ONE

"In the beginning there was God, the Eternal Father, the One Soul, the Oversoul, the source of all Light. And the Light begat other lights, other souls. I am one of those points of light, you are another point of light. I tell you we are all points of light, shining bright white, deep within. That is how it has always been. It is how it will always be."

—THE CHRONICLES OF THE SECOND COMING

Sunday, 4:42 a.m.

SISTER ANNUKKA CRADLED the book, her arms tightly wrapped around it. She hurried down hallways and up stairwells and didn't want to lose the book should she trip or fall. Footsteps echoed off in the distance, so she pushed herself to run faster. Someone was coming after her, chasing her through the early morning quiet of the monastery, growing closer with each passing minute.

She headed for the dormitory section, the hall where the acolytes slept. Several hours earlier she had prepared what might be a final message to her acolyte. She hated to place such a burden, her burden, onto another person. But there was no one else and there was no more time. When she found the room belonging to Summer, she slipped the note under the door, hoping the young woman would find it upon waking and honor her urgent requests.

Annukka made the quick dash between the dormitory and the Administration Building which housed the monastery's library. What better place to hide a book than in a room filled with books? A quick turn off the main hallway brought her to the rear entrance of the library and the shelves containing an extensive collection of Bibles. Without a second thought, she shoved the book in between two copies of the New Testament.

She prayed the book would find its way into safe hands, and then quickly left the library through a different door.

Sunday, 4:58 a.m.

ANNUKKA FELT HERSELF TIRING. She had not slept in almost twenty-four hours, and the running and the climbing of steps all served to deplete her energy. The detour through the library had not fooled her pursuer. She still heard footsteps and their unbroken pace. She doubted very much whoever it was had stopped to inspect the shelves of books. With the note and the book delivered, only escaping from the monastery remained. She hoped one last trick would lead her to freedom.

She burst through a set of double doors out into the chill early morning air and followed a brick pathway to the rear precinct wall of the monastery grounds. A small gate was there, half-hidden behind a clump of tall bushes. She had checked to make certain it was unlocked in the dimming glow of twilight.

Just as she found the bushes, the sounds of the double doors slamming shut and footsteps running straight toward her reverberated across the courtyard. Within seconds she arrived at the gate and reached to open the latch. Much to her horror, she found a chain wrapped around the edge of the gate and the iron post opposite its hinges. A lock held the chain in place.

She turned around, thinking she might evade her pursuer, but it was too late.

"So, you thought you might make your way out of here, did you?" said a man's voice, panting from the chase. "I'm sorry to disappoint you, Sister, but that exit is closed for the night."

Annukka saw her pursuer for the first time. He fought to catch his breath. Dressed in black, with a black substance smeared on his face and hands, his features remained hidden. He reached behind his back, produced a laze-gun, and aimed it at Annukka. Adrenaline shot through her body. There was no escaping.

"Now how about you tell me where the book is. Tell me and I might just let you live to see another sunrise."

"I'm not sure I know what you're talking about. What book?"

"Oh, come now, Sister. You know very well what book I'm after. If you don't tell me, I'll just have to kill you here and now. Then I'll retrace your steps until I find it. Some very important people on Old Earth want that book out of circulation, if you know what I mean."

Sister Annukka said nothing. She stood still, closed her eyes, and uttered a silent prayer to prepare herself for what she knew would be the final seconds of life.

"Well, Sister. What'll it be? The hot bite of my weapon, or the cold, hard stones of the monastery's prison cell?"

Please, dear God. Be with Acolyte Summer. Keep the book safe.

And then, without expression, the man raised the laze-gun and fired. A bright burst of orange fire shot out across the space between them and burned a hole straight through Sister Annukka's chest. She dropped to the ground. A red stain spread out from her now motionless body.

——— oOo ———

Sunday, 5:26 a.m.

THE BELLS SIGNALING THE CALL to Morning Prayer rang early. Summer opened her right eye and stared at the small clock. Five twenty-six. She closed her eye and drifted off to sleep again. The bells were not supposed to ring until seven o'clock. The bells continued to ring. Summer opened both eyes this time, her mind a little bit more engaged. Five forty-two.

Something must be wrong. Why else would someone put out a Call to Morning Prayer at such an hour? she concluded. Summer grudgingly threw back the warm covers and sat up. After stretching her arms out wide, she planted her feet on the cold floor, stood up, and made her way to her small bathroom. She relieved herself, ran some cold water over her face, tied her long blond hair back with an elastic band, and got dressed.

The bells continued to ring. *Yes,* she concluded. *Something is definitely wrong.*

——— o0o ———

Sunday, 5:57 a.m.

SUMMER FOUND HER WAY DOWN to the chapel. Other acolytes and sisters were arriving, most not quite yet awake. All confused about the early Call to Morning Prayer.

She found an empty pew at the back and slid halfway down its length on the off chance someone else might wish to share the row. The echoes of half-intelligible whispers filled the room.

The Mother Superior stood up and walked to the center of the dais. Dressed in her red robe, she was a beacon of color, presenting quite the contrast to the blacks and grays of the sisters and the acolytes. When she found her place, a quick glance off to the side signaled someone to cease the incessant ringing of the bells. All of the whispering stopped.

After making a silent prayer and the sign of the Cross, she began to speak. In her quiet voice, she said, "I'm sure you are all wondering why it is I have called you here at such an early hour. It is with a heavy heart I must inform you of the passing of Sister Annukka. And while this most unfortunate news could have waited for our morning gathering at its usual time, how our dear sister passed is what prompted me to call for an immediate gathering. Sister Annukka did not die of natural causes." The Mother Superior paused for a moment, waiting for the buzz of whispers to die down.

"Sister Annukka was murdered, right here on the monastery grounds." Another swell of murmuring arose. Another pause.

"Because this was a murder, and because it was committed on the grounds of our monastery, it is our responsibility to investigate this terrible thing and to try and identify the murderer. We don't know if someone here did it, though I can't imagine any of you being responsible, or if someone from town somehow made their way onto our grounds. But regardless, a bigger question, of course, is why someone would want to kill Sister Annukka." More whispering.

"So, I must now ask you to return to your rooms and remain there until a priest or monk can question you. It is my hope we can clear each of you from any responsibility. Then we will turn over the case to the authorities in town. Please be patient. When we are finished with our questioning, we will ring the bells for our morning meal."

The Mother Superior said a prayer, asking God to grant the peace that passes all understanding to Sister Annukka's soul and that He grant mercy for the one responsible for the Sister's death. After the conclusion of the prayer and the final "Amen," she dismissed everyone.

——— oOo ———

Sunday, 6:31 a.m.

WHEN SUMMER RETURNED TO her room, she opened the door and noticed a piece of paper on the floor just barely underneath her bed.

What is this? Why didn't I see it when I got up? Maybe the sleep in my eyes caused me to miss it, or maybe I could only see it now because of my different vantage point, she thought.

She bent over, picked it up, unfolded it, and began reading.

Summer,

I'm sorry I cannot deliver this request in person, but time is short. You must do something for me. You must go to the library and retrieve a very old and very valuable book. It is between copies of the New Testament, BS185 1987.228. You will know you have the right book because it will not have any call number on its spine. You must take this book to Father Bakkar, an old priest who lives in a little cottage out at the end of Paladin Lane, out at the edge of town. He will know what to do with it. But you must not tell anyone about the book. I know I'm asking a lot, but it is of the utmost importance you deliver this book as quickly as possible. The future of our religion depends on it. May the Good Lord bless you and keep you.

Annukka

"Oh, my goodness! She must have slid this under my door before . . . before . . . she was murdered. Oh, my goodness!"

Summer's heart beat faster as questions popped into her mind. *Was Annukka killed because of what she hid in the library? Was someone after this book? What could be so important it was worth killing for, worth dying for?* A shudder ran up and down her spine. *If I am to do as Sister Annukka asked, will whoever killed her be after me?* Summer closed the door and sat down on the corner of her bed.

"This is serious," she whispered aloud, "very serious. I don't know what's happening here. We are all supposed to remain in our rooms, wait for someone to come and question us. If I'm not here when that someone shows up, I will be in trouble, perhaps big trouble. They might even think I was responsible for Annukka's murder. If I leave this room and make my way to the library undetected, retrieve this book, and sneak out of the monastery, I will, quite likely, never be able to return. But what if I stay and they, whoever 'they' are, discover Annukka was outside my room and that she left me a note. Then what? And if I don't leave now, this very instant, I may never have the chance to. And this book? What will happen to it?"

Instinct told her to go to the library immediately. Maybe with all of the commotion at the monastery this morning and everyone trying to figure out who might have murdered Sister Annukka, maybe she could do this. Maybe, maybe, maybe. Her head screamed with doubts.

Please, dear God, give me strength. Guide my path.

Summer got up, grabbed her satchel, tucked the note into the outer pocket, and wrapped her cloak around her shoulders. She quietly closed her door and left the dormitory.

Sunday, 6:59 a.m.

THE ONLY LIGHT IN THE STILL-DARK office emanated from a computer screen. The featureless silhouette in the center of the display spoke in hushed tones.

"You need to secure the book and you need to do it before whoever has it disappears from our grasp."

"I know. And I'm sorry Sister Annukka did not have the book in her possession when we caught her."

"It is most unfortunate you disposed of the good sister before you learned of the book's whereabouts. Our superiors will find that most regrettable."

"I understand. Please assure them I will make every effort to find the book and anyone else who might have helped Sister Annukka."

"Make certain you do. You will not be given a second chance."

The screen went dark. The viewer sat in silence in the darkened office, trying desperately to figure out what her next move should be.

Sunday, 7:03 a.m.

SUMMER'S CLOAK WAS JUST DARK enough to provide her with cover as she sped across the courtyard between the dormitory and the Administration Building. She wondered why no one was out. But it was still early and dark. Perhaps the parties investigating Annukka's murder were preoccupied. But no matter.

She entered the Administration Building through a

side door and made her way up to the second floor. She wished she had spent more time studying in the library and had more familiarity with its layout. But following the call numbers prominently posted at the end of each row of books eventually led her to the shelf containing all of the Bibles. Annukka's note had said the book would be with the New Testaments with the call numbers of BS185 1987.228. Summer's pace slowed as she zeroed in on the appropriate section. She ran her index finger along the spines of books on one shelf after another until she found her target.

Because of the dim light, she couldn't quite see the call numbers. But it was too risky to turn on any lights. She continued running her index finger along the spines of the various editions of the New Testament, thinking perhaps she could feel what she could not see.

Then there was a gap between two tall books. Pushing them apart, she found a smaller leather-bound book. She pulled it out and turned it over in her hands. The note said there would be no call number on the spine. A flash of excitement shot through her. There was no call number and the book definitely looked old. She quickly opened it to check the title. Sister Annukka had not mentioned the title but did say the future of their religion would depend on this book.

The spine protested a bit as she opened it. She read the title page. *The Chronicles of the Second Coming.* The words were handwritten in flowing calligraphy on parchment that was discolored, containing several dark patches and ragged edges.

What? Was this real? She had heard rumors of a Second Coming. But that was hundreds of years ago on Old Earth. How did such a book come to be on Solus II?

Based on the title, Summer started to realize the significance of Annukka's note. Yes, perhaps this really was an important book.

She carefully placed the book in her satchel, pushed together the books on each side of her find, and made her way out of the library and down a back stairwell.

She opened the back door just a crack to see if her intended path was clear. But there were voices coming from the back corner of the courtyard, the corner where an old iron gate led out to town. She froze. The gate was her only means of getting out of the monastery unnoticed. Any other entryway would be too visible. And now that she had the book, she most certainly could not take any unnecessary risks.

Her intuition told her to wait for a few moments. The voices were from two or three men. They seemed to be moving from the gate along the back precinct wall of the monastery. After another minute or two, Summer opened the door just a bit more and peered to her right. No one was at the back gate. She looked to the left and saw the men. They were dragging something along the ground. A wave of nausea overtook Summer. It was Annukka's body.

Wait just a bit longer, she told herself, just long enough for the men to leave the courtyard, but not one second longer. The horizon was starting to lose its blackness, turning a dark blue. The star around which Solus II orbited would be up within the hour.

As soon as the men were out of sight, Summer quietly opened and closed the door, so it didn't slam shut. She followed the backside of the Administration Building for as long as possible, then headed out across the courtyard to the back corner and the gate.

The grove of bushes provided her with cover and a short respite to catch her breath. A wave of panic rippled through her body when she reached for the iron gate. A chain wound its way around one side of the gate and the post opposite the hinges. It took a moment for Summer to notice a portion of the chain was melted. And those links were covered with blood.

This must be where Annukka was killed, she thought. *The energy bolt must have passed through Annukka's body and struck the chain. It was the only explanation.*

Summer pulled at the chain, twisting and turning the still-warm section until one of the links snapped, enabling her to push open the gate. Stepping through the gateway gave her a feeling of victory. The gate swung shut behind her as she took off into the backstreets of the town. Now she needed some time to think and to come up with a plan before locating this Father Bakkar. And she knew just where to go.

TWO

"The Source of all Light is God, the Eternal Father, the One Soul, the Oversoul. It is from this source each and every soul originates, each and every soul a product of its light and its love."

—THE CHRONICLES OF THE SECOND COMING

Sunday, 8:23 a.m.

DANCER SAT AT HER KITCHEN TABLE, a sturdy butcher block piece of furniture she purchased from a local pawn shop several years back. Piles of paper covered the table, each pile a portion of a script for a stage play opening at the local theater. She had won her first lead role, but memorizing the lines was proving to be difficult.

She smiled at the irony of the show's title. *The Last Sunday of Summer.* What would her twin sister think? And why had her parents given her and her sister the names they had? Dancer? She was no dancer. An actress, maybe. And Summer? Her sister wasn't even born in summer. She laughed and turned the page, reciting the next block of lines from memory.

A hurried knock on her apartment door broke her concentration. She got up and made her way across the living room.

"Who's there?" she said, always a bit cautious before opening the door.

"It's Summer," came the reply. "Let me in! And be quick about it!"

Dancer unbolted the door and opened it, surprised to see Summer standing there, out-of-breath and clutching a leather satchel. "Come in, come in."

As soon as Summer entered the room, Dancer shut the door and slid the bolt back into place.

"What in the world? You look like you've been running. Is everything okay?"

Summer placed her bundle down on one of the chairs and immediately started to disrobe. "Do you have some spare clothes I might borrow?"

"Sure, but . . ."

"No time to explain right now. I need to disguise myself. Do you have a scarf or something I can wrap around my head?"

"Okay, okay. Give me a second." Dancer retreated into her bedroom and returned a minute later with clothes, shoes, and a headdress.

Summer finished disrobing and pulled on the clothes Dancer picked out for her. She bundled up her acolyte's robe and gave it to Dancer, then said, "Great. Now take my uniform and hide it somewhere, just in case anyone followed me here. I don't want them to recognize me."

Dancer took the bundle and headed off to her bedroom. She placed the clothes in a dresser drawer and then covered them over with socks and underwear. Hurrying back to the living room, she said, "Okay. Now would you kindly tell me what the heck is going on? I don't see you for months at a time, and now you come blowing in here like the world's on fire."

"I know, I know. I'm sorry. Okay." Summer took a deep breath and exhaled. "Did you ever hear stories from Old Earth about a man who claimed to be the Second Coming of Jesus Christ?" Summer asked as she nervously paced back and forth across Dancer's living room.

"Of course, I did. The Church cried heresy and shunned him, claimed his miracles were tricks and not the works of a divine God."

"And do you recall what happened to him?"

"He disappeared without a trace. Some say he was killed. Some say he really was a fake, and he simply went into hiding."

"What if I told you he might not have been a fake, that maybe he really was who he claimed to be?"

"And why would you say that? That was a long time ago. What proof do you have?"

Summer reached for her satchel and pulled out an oblong object. She unwrapped the piece of worn leather and held out the small book.

"What's that?" Dancer asked.

"*The Chronicles of the Second Coming*," said Summer very matter-of-factly. "I just came into its possession earlier this morning. I haven't read it, mind you. But based on the events at the monastery this morning . . ."

"You're kidding, right?"

"No. I'm quite serious."

"And just how in the world did you come to have this book in your possession?"

"Well, that is *the* question, isn't it?"

Summer walked over to the sofa where her sister sat, placed the book back in its wrapping, and explained.

"This morning, just before five o'clock, the bells for Morning Prayer started ringing."

Dancer interrupted, "Isn't five o'clock a bit early?"

"It is. So, after I got myself out of bed and dressed, I headed down to the chapel, as did all of the other Sisters and acolytes. After we were all there, the Mother Superior announced Sister Annukka, my mentor, had been murdered."

"What? Murders don't happen in monasteries, do they?"

"Apparently, they do," continued Summer. "She then proceeded to dismiss us, ordering that we were all to remain confined to our rooms until further notice. She initiated an investigation. She said we were all to be questioned. She expressed concern the person who committed the murder might be a resident of the monastery."

"Okay. This is all getting pretty strange. But what does that have to do with the book?"

"Yes, the book . . ." Summer placed her hands on the bundle in her lap. "When I returned to my room, I noticed a piece of paper near the door. I hadn't seen it when I got up, probably due to my sleep-filled eyes or my vantage point, but someone slid it under my door while I was asleep. I think Sister Annukka wrote the note before she was killed."

"Do you still have the note? Can I see it?"

Summer retrieved the folded-up piece of paper from the satchel, unfolded it, and handed it to Dancer.

"So, she wanted you to go to the library, find the book, and get it away from the monastery?"

"Yep. I can only assume Annukka trusted me enough to follow through on whatever mission she was unable to complete."

"And what mission would that be?" queried Dancer.

"I'm not certain. I think that's why the good Sister directed me to seek out this priest. I'm not certain if she meant for me to give the book to this fellow or what. But I do think she wrote the note in a hurry, and she didn't have time to fully explain her intentions."

"Wow, so what are you going to do?" Dancer took a deep breath and sighed.

"Yes, well, without any way to independently verify this book really is what it is supposed to be, and knowing Sister Annukka lost her life trying to get it out of the monastery, I think this is some pretty serious business. Whoever killed Sister Annukka could well be after me now. It won't take too long before someone at the monastery notices my absence and comes looking for me. And if they remember I have a sister who lives nearby, they may well come looking for me here."

Dancer's face changed with the realization her sister's actions put her at risk, too.

"I'm really sorry, Dancer. I know this puts you in danger. I didn't mean to. But I had nowhere else to go. I needed some time to think about what to do," Summer said, wiping away tears.

"Okay. It's too late to change things. What's done is done. Your pursuers would have likely shown up here anyway looking for you. Not to worry. I'm your sister and I will do whatever I need to do to help you."

"Thank you. I figured I could count on you."

"We need a plan, though, some way to divert anyone who might have followed you here, or at least remembered you have a sister and that I live in town. And then there is the book. We need to get it to this priest fellow and to get you uninvolved somehow. Get you safe."

—— oOo ——

Sunday, 9:00 a.m.

"PROGRESS REPORT," THE ANONYMOUS figure on the computer screen said with little hint of professionalism or politeness.

"Our investigators have been systematically interviewing all of the Sisters and the acolytes. So far, the only anomaly is the disappearance of one of our acolytes. Summer is her name. We went to her room and found it empty. Nothing was missing except her cloak. We checked our records. She had been the acolyte of Sister Annukka for her first year here. We're not certain if there's a connection."

"And she's not anywhere on the grounds?"

"While we haven't done a thorough search as of this minute, she is certainly not anywhere visible. Security cameras didn't pick up anything. No one left the grounds."

"Assuming she is nowhere in the monastery, where would she have gone?"

"We're checking into that, as well. According to the paperwork she filled out upon being accepted as an acolyte two years ago, she has a sister who lives on Solus, in the local settlement. Our security logs show Summer has visited her sister several times during her time here."

"I think it prudent you check all leads, including paying a visit to her sister. But I remind you to be discreet. We do not want to create any incident causing local authorities to wonder what we're up to. We must keep our search for the book out of the public domain. Do not contact the local authorities until I give you my approval."

"Yes. I understand."

"I do hope you have something more substantial to report when you check in next time. We are counting on you."

"Understood."

The screen went dead. Darkness once again surrounded its solitary occupant.

She picked up the telephone, dialed in a series of numbers, and listened for an answer.

"Yes?" came a quick response.

"I need you to do something for me."

——— oOo ———

Sunday, 9:20 a.m.

"I HAVE AN IDEA," SAID DANCER matter-of-factly. "I'm just curious. You said the folks at the monastery know about me, know you have a twin sister?"

"Yes. They were pretty thorough in their questioning before they accepted my application. One of the sections dealt with family relationships, family ties. They wanted to make certain I wasn't trying to escape from something or someone. And they wanted to make certain my desire to join the Sisterhood and serve the Church didn't go against someone's wishes. Since Mom and Dad are no longer with us, I guess they didn't bother to ask you for your permission."

"Which I would have given, naturally," inserted Dancer.

"I know. So, yes, they know I have a sister living close by."

"Hmmm. Well, maybe whoever is in charge of the investigation doesn't know that or hasn't figured out you're part of this deepening drama. Maybe we can use this to our advantage."

"Okay. What are you talking about?"

"Let's say you were being followed here. And let's say someone is watching my apartment to see if you leave. Or maybe the someones didn't follow you here and are not watching my place but have lookouts in town watching out for you. Either way, they are looking for you dressed in your acolyte garb, with your cloak. What would happen if we gave them what they wanted?"

"What? Are you crazy?" exclaimed Summer.

"I'm your twin sister, remember? What if I dressed up in your attire and headed out in one direction? Then, after a while you, in civilian clothes, and with the book, of course, head out in a different direction? Out to the edge of town?"

"I hear you. It's a great plan except for one small detail. It puts you in terrible danger. So, no. We can't do that," Summer objected.

"What if I took something resembling your satchel with me and put an extra set of clothes inside it. Then, after fifteen minutes of walking in the wrong direction, I duck into someplace where I change clothes and head out a back entrance? Then I could make my way out to this Father Bakkar fellow via a different path and meet up with you?"

"I dunno. I'm not sure I like it." Summer shook her head from side to side.

"Do you have a better plan?" asked Dancer.

Summer sat in silence, still shaking her head.

"Sister, dear, remember two things. First, Mom and Dad never could tell us apart. And if they couldn't, neither will anyone else. And second—need I remind you—I am an actress? Let me act. And I know the person I am portraying really well! It's a good plan. It will work. I'm going to go and retrieve your acolyte uniform. While I change, take a few minutes to rest up, eat something. There's some freshly baked bread and your favorite strawberry jam in the kitchen. And then we'll figure out our respective paths. Okay?"

"I reluctantly agree. But only because I can't think of a better plan. But Dancer, this is serious stuff. We don't know how things will go. You may not be able to return to your wonderful little apartment after this. Make sure you're really and truly okay with this."

"Look, if the folks at the monastery know about me, and they're desperate to get their hands on this book, I'm not safe here anyway. And it's too late to do anything about that."

"Well, as usual, you're right." Summer tugged on her left ring finger and extended an open hand toward her sister. "Here. If they should stop you and you need to convince them you are me, this ring will help. All acolytes wear them. It's only if they ask to see your left wrist." Summer pulled up her left sleeve and displayed a small tattoo of a cross. "You'll be in trouble. You won't have the tattoo. Then they will know you are, in fact, not me. Not sure if that's a bad thing or a good thing. It might just save your life. You will have to think on your feet and be the judge of how to play things. You've always been good at that sort of thing. Just be careful."

"Got it. Now let's get ourselves together, shall we?"

Dancer retreated to her bedroom, thinking to herself, *Well, the good news is, I may not have to worry about memorizing my lines anymore.*

THREE

"Our collection of light-souls drifted through your galaxy for billions of years until we found your most unique planet. We decided it worthy of further development, and so, with the force of our collective energies, we began to move molecules, to create amino acids and DNA. And that process eventually gave rise to life and caused the evolution of the sentient beings now on your world."
—THE CHRONICLES OF THE SECOND COMING

Sunday, 1:27 p.m.

THE OLD PRIEST STOOD IN HIS kitchen making a cup of tea. The kettle sang its high-pitched whistle. He poured the steaming hot water into his ceramic mug and allowed the tea to steep for a few minutes. He looked out the dining room window at the bleak landscape of Solus II. Centuries of terraforming had done wonders for the atmosphere and the climate. But increasing the population of trees was still something the climatologists had yet to achieve.

After removing the teabag, he submerged a spoonful of local honey into the mug and stirred several times. He blew on the tea, hoping to cool it a bit before his first sip. A quick taste confirmed the correct amount of honey had been added.

As he left the kitchen, there was a knock on his front door. He set the mug down and shuffled across the room to see who had come to visit him.

"Hello?" he said after opening the door. A pretty young woman dressed in plain clothes and clutching a satchel stood on his porch. "May I help you?"

"Are you the priest from Old Earth, Father Bakkar?" she asked. "Because if you are, I am here to say you may well be in great danger." Summer made a quick assessment of this individual Annukka requested she find. His face was kind but showed his age, his hair was gray, and he still wore the traditional clerical collar. A silver chain with a small wooden cross hung around his neck.

"And who are you, young lady?" queried the Old Priest.

"My name is Summer. Acolyte Summer. From the monastery. And I have news regarding Sister Annukka and," she quickly looked to her right and then to her left, "and the book. May I come in?"

Summer saw a look of surprise on the face of the Old Priest. All color left his wrinkled face. Perhaps it was because she mentioned Sister Annukka's name. Or maybe because she mentioned the book.

"Yes, yes. Come in, child," said the Old Priest with a sense of urgency in his voice.

Summer entered the sparsely decorated cottage as the priest quickly closed the door.

"Please, sit. Can I get you something?"

"No. I'm fine, thank you."

"Give me a minute." The old man collected his still-warm tea and then sat down.

"Now, child, tell me what it is you have come to tell me."

"There is so much to say and so little time to say it in, so I will get to the point right away."

"Okay," uttered the Old Priest.

"Sister Annukka was murdered at the monastery early this morning."

"What? How?"

"When I left the monastery earlier today, I had not received word regarding who might be responsible for her death or exactly how she was killed, though I suspect someone shot her with a laze-gun. Before she was killed, she left me a note. And in the note, Sister Annukka asked me to do two things. The first was to go to the library and retrieve this book which she had hidden there." Summer opened her satchel and produced the bundle containing the book. "And the second thing she requested was I find you and deliver the book to you."

Summer paused for a moment, then said, "I'm to assume you know what this is all about? Besides the note the Sister left me, and after a quick look inside the book, I can only guess at what is happening. Perhaps you might enlighten me a bit?"

The priest took a long sip from his tea, then started to tell his story.

"I am, indeed, from Earth. You were right about that," he began. "I worked in Vatican City, for the Pope himself. During the years of my service, I became aware of many things, some of which were things not known to the faithful. The Church has many secrets, you know?

"Late one night, a priest paid me a visit at my apartment. He told me of the growing tension between those insistent the Church maintain its rule over the Outer Worlds and those distant clergy who wanted to break with the earth-bound religion. The schism started when word of the so-called Second Coming of our Savior reached the Off-Worlders. Seems as though they believed the person who claimed to be the reincarnation of the Messiah was indeed who he said he was. Not everyone in the Vatican was convinced. In fact, very few were. How Off-Worlders learned of this event is not known, especially because the Vatican did everything it could to squelch the story."

Summer sat motionless, fascinated she was privy to a story not known by followers of the faith, whether they be on Earth or Off-World.

The Old Priest continued, "But what no one knew is that this so-called Second Savior wrote a book. Some refer to as the Third Testament of the Bible or the Chronicles of the Second Coming. And in that book, he detailed the exact nature of God, the universe, heaven, the afterlife, and the purpose of his first incarnation on Earth. The book explains how the initial teachings of Jesus were, to use an unfortunate descriptor, dumbed down so that the peoples of the time, who were mostly poor and uneducated, might better understand the messages being taught. This fellow who claimed to be the reincarnation of Christ wanted everyone to know how things really worked, now that most human beings were highly educated, and the human race had a much better understanding of science and the universe."

"And this book," Summer said as she unwrapped the bundle, "is that book?"

"Yes," replied the priest, nodding his head up and down. "That book is a threat to the Church. There are those in high places on Earth who do not want its contents to be revealed to anyone, especially to the Outer Worlds. The Vatican believes, rightly or wrongly, this book would give those wanting to solidify their break from the Church the ammunition they need to convince folks to believe in a New Faith, a religion more in line with science and the message of this Second Savior, and less on the traditional teachings that God offers human beings salvation and eternal life through the Crucifixion of Christ and His subsequent resurrection."

"And how did you come to have possession of this book?" asked Summer.

"This visitor I mentioned, the priest, the one who first told me of the book, what it said, why it was so important, and why it was its contents must be made public . . ."

"Yes, but why did he visit *you* and tell you all of this? Surely there were others he could have entrusted with all of this."

"True enough, child." The Old Priest finished his tea and set the mug down on the end table next to his chair. "The answer is quite simple. I was past my prime. My career was winding down. I had not made any enemies in the Church. I kept to myself. And here is the most important thing. I had access to the room where the book was hidden. This priest somehow knew that about me. And he knew the exact location of the book.

"And so, what this fellow wanted was for me to steal the book and to take it Off-World, to deliver it to the Mother Superior on Vatican Prime. And so I did. I stole it. After securing the book, I quietly slipped away to the nearest spaceport and bought a ticket on a sleeper ship to here, Solus II."

"But what about Vatican Prime?"

"I know, I know. After I obtained the book, I found there were no flights heading out to Vatican Prime for several months. And I had to get off Earth, get the book off Earth as quickly as possible. So here I am. When I got here, I lived at the monastery for several years, getting to know the Sisters, looking for one to whom I might entrust the book and my mission."

"And that person was Sister Annukka?"

"Exactly."

"And she was supposed to get the book to Vatican Prime?"

"Yes. But something must have happened. Someone must have become suspicious of the Sister, or perhaps learned of the book and its presence on Solus II. But whatever happened, it caused her to reach out to you and ask you to carry out the mission."

"Well, if you are indeed the person who carried the book from Earth to Solus II, then I'm happy to give it back to you and relieve myself of this burden."

"No. I don't think you understand. You are now the one who must carry the book and deliver it to Vatican Prime."

"Oh, no. I'm not going to any such place. I have my twin sister here, and I have my life, and . . ."

"You have nothing here. Not anymore. You cannot go back to the monastery. They will know what you have done. They will imprison you or kill you. The powers that be will not let you go. You know too much."

"No!" Summer protested. "I am not going to get on some sleeper ship and spend decades in space just to deliver a book to folks seeking to establish a new religion I don't even fully understand. This was your mission, not mine."

"I am too old to go through another cycle of deep sleep. A ship captain would never permit me to take such a flight if he knew my age or that I had already spent decades in a deep sleep. No, it must be you. We do not . . . I do not have time to find another. The individual or individuals who killed Sister Annukka will be looking for you, for us. And if they find the book, the book documenting the teachings of the Second Savior, it will be lost forever."

Summer thought about the supposed Second Coming and that the author of this book might just be the reincarnation of the very Savior to whom she had hoped to commit her life. And within several hours, she went from being a lowly, insignificant acolyte to perhaps playing a significant role in the history of the Church, whether it be the Old Church or some New Faith yet to solidify on the Outer Worlds. Was her life on Solus II really so important she would turn down a chance to be a part of history? To be a person of significance?

"Okay," she finally said, "if I am to commit my life to your cause, I need some more answers. Do you believe any of this story about the Second Savior?"

"I do," replied the Old Priest.

"Why?"

"There is a second part to the story of this Second Savior, the proof of which could not easily be brought Off-World. Not like the book. You see, the Church had this Second Savior arrested and tried him on charges of heresy. They sentenced him to death. But when the guards went to escort him to be executed, they found him gone. And in his cell was this book."

Summer's eyes widened. Her grip on the book tightened.

The Old Priest paused for a moment, crossed himself, then said, "The Church also found the image of this man burned onto the sheet covering his bed. The image was almost a perfect replica of the Shroud of Turin, a second shroud, if you will."

"And this shroud is what you couldn't bring Off-World with you?" asked Summer.

"Right. The Church sealed the sheet between two pieces of plexiglass. It would have been a bit difficult for me to sneak out of the basement vault with something so big," the old man said with a bit of a laugh.

"Okay, so you're convinced this Second Savior authored this book. And you're telling me the Church was afraid it would lose its influence if any of this story were widely known. Funny how history repeated itself. God sends us the messenger we pray for and what do we do to the messenger? We kill him. So sad. Makes one wonder why we aspire for perfection when all we do is shun those who achieve it. Perhaps because it makes the rest of us look bad?" The young acolyte sat quietly, shaking her head.

"You have stated the cold, hard truth. That's the irony of the Church and what it's all about. I also wonder if humanity will ever change. Seems as though our worst qualities follow us wherever we go, even out to the stars."

"I appreciate you telling me all of this. I suppose it is now up to me to pass on this story and the book to those on Vatican Prime. Now I need to know just how exactly it is I'm supposed to get to Vatican Prime."

"Good point," said the priest. "I have a contact at the spaceport. These days, it's not uncommon for there to be at least two or three ships on planet. And because I do keep track of the comings and goings of these ships, I know there's a ship in port right now. The *Veritas*, I believe. It's heading for Vatican Prime in the next day or two." The old man stopped in mid-sentence, cocked his head a bit, raised his hand to his chin, and finally continued. "You know? I wonder if the presence of that ship isn't what caused Sister Annukka to make plans to leave the monastery, and someone realized what she was up to. Perhaps even knew why. Yes, that might explain the timing of events."

"Okay. That helps a little. Just exactly how do I pay for a ticket? Trips like that are outrageously expensive, are they not?"

"I have means, young one. You will have to trust me. All will be provided for you." The Old Priest got up and walked back to his study, returning with an envelope. He handed it to Summer, then sat back down. "In that envelope is everything you need to secure passage on the *Veritas*. Give it to the captain when you board the ship. There is also a note in there giving him certain instructions, the most important of which is to be discreet, to keep your presence a secret, and not to mention your name on the flight plan."

"Okay, so one more thing," started Summer. "The only reason I was able to make my way to your house was because of my sister, my twin sister, Dancer. She came up with a plan to divert anyone who might have followed me from the monastery. She donned my acolyte uniform and left her apartment before me, heading for the Rail Station, hoping to entice anyone looking for me to follow her. Before she left, I gave her your address. After a sufficient amount of time, she was to have changed into civilian garb and head here. She doesn't know I'm headed for the spaceport. If she should appear at your doorstep after I leave, please instruct her how to find me. And see what you can do about securing passage for her, as well. The thought of leaving her behind is more painful than anything. And, if everything you said is true, she probably won't be able to return to her life here on Solus II either."

"Of course. It is the least I can do for you. Thank you, young lady, for your sacrifice. One day, all of this will be taught to the young children of the New Faith.

"And one more thing," added the priest, "I will send a message to my contact on Vatican Prime and let them know the events of today and that they will be receiving a visitor in about thirty years, along with one very important book."

"Visitor? Really? I doubt very much I will ever make another trek across the stars in my lifetime. Most certainly not my idea of fun."

FOUR

"Once our collection of light-souls had guided the evolution of life to the point when creatures capable of intelligent thought appeared, we found ourselves able to enter their bodies and their minds and live within them and through them for periods lasting years. When their bodies would wear themselves out or become sick, our light-souls returned to our collective and await another opportunity to experience life on your world."

—THE CHRONICLES OF THE SECOND COMING

VATICAN PRIME SERVED AS the center of the Holy Catholic Church for all of the Outer Worlds. The planet orbited Teegarden's Star, an M-type red dwarf sun approximately twelve light-years from Old Earth. The early interstellar explorers deemed it a target of interest because of its location in the habitable zone of its host sun and because Teegarden's Star did not emit powerful solar flares, something characteristic of many red dwarf stars.

It took several centuries to colonize the planet and enrich its atmosphere with oxygen from plants brought from Earth. And it took several more centuries after humankind's reach out into the stars for the Holy See to realize their declining influence on the Outer Worlds. There were those in the Church who saw man's continual expansion to Earth-like exoplanets to be a threat to its ability to govern the faithful. They feared the great distances between the Vatican City-State on Earth and human settlements would somehow diminish the allegiance of parishioners to the Church.

But some were more forward-thinking. They thought keeping the faith centralized on Earth would, sooner or later, lead to the severing of all ties between the Church and what would surely become a more dominant interstellar society. In an effort to prevent this, they proposed the establishment of a series of consulates, one on each Earth-like exoplanet. But the traditionalists rejected the idea.

The appearance of an individual on Old Earth claiming to be the reincarnation of Jesus Christ and spreading his teachings about who and what God really is and how the universe really works only served to increase the tension between the Old Church and the Off-World Church. The powers in Vatican City felt threatened by this individual, and, like the Sanhedrin in the days leading up to the Crucifixion, they moved to silence this new voice.

With the permission of the Pope, the Church Elders devised a scheme to lure the so-called Second Savior away from his followers. This individual was quickly and quietly captured, imprisoned, and sentenced to death by the Vatican Court of First Instance. The morning of the execution came, and members of the Pontifical Gendarmerie arrived at the cell to escort its habitant to the room where the sentence was to be carried out. Much to the surprise of the guards, they found the jail cell empty. No one could explain how or when this individual escaped. The security cameras did not reveal anything except a brief flash of light at exactly midnight.

But what the Church Elders who came to examine the cell did find was a book resting prominently in the middle of the pillow on the cell's one bed, as well as an imprint of a man on the bed's solitary sheet, complete with a man's face and beard and the man's hands folded across his chest. The Church Elders stared blankly at one another and whispered, "A second shroud? No. It can't be! Perhaps this man truly was the reincarnation of our Savior!"

The Church discreetly removed the sheet and preserved it between two panes of plexiglass. The Cardinals closest to the Pope studied the book and, had it not been for the image on the sheet, the book would have been declared to be a work of pure fiction, if not heresy. The Pope decreed the two items should be locked away in the most secret of places within the Vatican's basement. The Church released a statement to the press saying this so-called Second Savior had disappeared and was quite likely a fraud. The story soon dropped off the main pages of internet news, but conspiracy theories ran amuck for years.

And all the while, the schism between those proposing an expansion of the Church and those wishing to stay tied to a single planet continued to grow. It soon became apparent to those supporting expansion that the only way to address the situation was to leave Earth and break away from the Church. The faction eventually did leave Earth and selected the colony on Teegarden c as its destination.

Upon their arrival, they began the construction of a second Vatican City.

As the centuries slipped by and the number of human beings living on various planets increased, so did the influence of this Second Vatican. And with time, the religion on the Outer Worlds, the religion once known as Catholicism with all of its beliefs and traditions, began to change, giving way to a more transcendental movement, one centered around God, the Eternal Father, the One Soul, the Oversoul. The keepers of this New Faith, the former Sisterhood, took on the title of Mothersouls.

There were those on Old Earth who were sympathetic to this New Faith, including one of the Pope's very own trusted assistants. The assistant, who knew of the ill-fated Second Savior, realized the beliefs of this New Faith matched many of the ideas put forth in the book found in the cell. He thought if this book could be delivered to the Off-World Church, it could well serve as a foundation for their faith, much as the Bible had been the cornerstone for the Catholic Church on Earth.

This assistant searched for someone he could trust to carry the book out to the stars, to the ever-growing colony on the newly named Vatican Prime. Then he found the Old Priest, someone no one would miss or think to question his disappearance. So, he told the Old Priest where to find the book and charged him with getting it Off-World, getting it to Vatican Prime.

He prayed he had done the right thing, prayed he had, perhaps, done the work of God, the Eternal Father, the One Soul, the Oversoul.

——— o0o ———

The trip from Earth to Solus II lasted forty-five years. When the priest awoke, he found himself on an unfamiliar world, a world which was the last of the Outer Worlds to be clinging to the teachings of Catholicism. *Perhaps this was a good thing*, he thought. He found his way to a monastery located in the center of the main settlement on the planet and quietly settled into his new life, all the while looking for someone with whom he could share his secret, someone with whom he could share the reason for his presence there.

FIVE

"Faith, my dear followers. Faith is everything. Faith is the earthly manifestation of the power the light-souls use to move molecules, to build worlds, to create life. The power hiding in one person's faith is indeed small, but when two or more gather together, that power is multiplied. And the more individuals there are praying for the same outcome, the more likely it is that outcome will occur. It was written that 'according to your faith, be it unto you.' I am here to tell you this is a true statement. So have faith. Use it to achieve all things great."
—THE CHRONICLES OF THE SECOND COMING

Sunday, 12:35 p.m.

DANCER ZIGZAGGED HER WAY through the streets and back alleys of the town. She set a quick pace for herself and made every effort to stay close to the buildings. Summer's cloak covered the top part of her face. She avoided eye contact with passersby.

For twenty minutes, she did her best to confuse anyone who might be following her or watching her. As she made way across town, she thought about where she might go to change clothes. Perhaps the best place for an acolyte to hide might be a church or a chapel. Changing directions yet again, she headed for a small chapel she attended from time to time. She knew there was a restroom off the narthex where she could change her attire. But she didn't know if the chapel had a rear entrance. *One thing at a time.*

Another block or two and the chapel came into view. Its white walls and aquamarine roof made it stand out from all of the other buildings surrounding it. Atop its steeple was an angel with wings unfurled and arms outstretched toward the heavens. The front door was propped open, and the sounds of people singing flowed out into the street. *Oh, this is perfect*, thought Dancer.

Upon entry, she found the ladies restroom, ducked into the stall farthest from the door, pulled off the acolyte garb, put on her change of clothes, and then stuffed Summer's uniform into the small bag. She exited the stall, dumped the bag into the trash can, and stepped out of the restroom to join the worship service.

After the final song and the benediction, the parishioners began to greet one another and find their way to the exit. Dancer fell in behind an elderly couple, acting as if she was a daughter or a personal care aide, making certain they wouldn't fall as they navigated their way down the steps in front of the chapel. Once outside, she followed them for a block before turning down another alleyway and heading off toward the Old Priest's residence.

——— o0o ———

Sunday, 2:00 p.m.

THE OLD PRIEST WATCHED OUT HIS living room window as Summer disappeared down the street leading out toward the spaceport. Once he lost sight of her, he closed the curtain, returned to his study, and clicked on his computer, bringing it back to life. He opened up a video-link and waited for a reply.

When he saw the face of the Mother Superior on his screen, he plainly said, "Progress report."

"I received word several minutes ago that Acolyte Summer left her sister's apartment and headed out across town. My contact followed her until she entered the local chapel. The midday service was almost at an end when she went in. My contact watched the parishioners leave the service but did not see Summer exit the premises. So, he went in and searched the building. Unfortunately, he didn't find any trace of her. It's obvious the young lady is clever. No doubt, she had a change of clothes with her and left when the service concluded. She could be anywhere in town by now."

The Old Priest thought to himself, *Good, Summer's plan worked perfectly. The Mother Superior's agent took the bait. Dancer should be on her way here now.*

"What is your next course of action?"

"Summer was heading toward the Rail Station before she went into the chapel. Perhaps she is hoping to catch a train destined for one of the outlying settlements and lay low for a while."

"Okay. Send your contacts to the Rail Station and watch it closely. She isn't wearing her acolyte robe any longer, so look for any young woman. Question them if you have to. Do not let her slip away again."

"Understood."

The Old Priest terminated the call. He wondered how much longer he could keep up his deception, how much longer he could pretend to be a representative of the Pope assigned to Solus II and continue to threaten the Mother Superior if she failed to retrieve the book. Well, no matter. Summer and the book would be safely Off-World and on their way to Vatican Prime by day's end before the good Mother Superior realized she'd been deceived. He wondered how much longer it would be before the men who had killed Annukka would come looking for him.

But the deception had served its purpose. It was the only way, the only recourse, he could think of to make up for his one fatal error. The error setting this whole terrible course of events into motion. The error leading to Annukka's untimely demise, to Summer's sacrifice, and perhaps the life of her sister.

His message to Annukka had been simple. The code word they agreed upon when he passed on responsibility for the mission to the good sister was "ire." In Latin, the dead language some in the Church still clung to, it meant "go." Perhaps that was too obvious. But the priest never fancied himself as the cloak and dagger type, someone who had any talent for secret missions.

Perhaps his message to Sister Annukka had been intercepted. Maybe he should have delivered word of the arrival of the *Veritas* in person rather than by email. Someone could have become suspicious when she went to retrieve the book from wherever she had it hidden. Or maybe someone figured out Annukka was making plans to flee from the monastery. But whatever it was, he knew his action had precipitated all of this.

Hopefully, this deception might secure safe passage for the book, he thought. And he would stay here in his little cottage. If the men came for him, maybe his sacrifice would buy him some forgiveness from Annukka's spirit, and from Summer, and Dancer, and from the priest who charged him with the mission back on Earth all those many years ago.

He switched back on his computer, initiated an interstellar communications link, then typed a quick message to the Mothersoul Superior on Vatican Prime.

"The package is on its way. Watch out for Summer."

The Old Priest went to wait for the arrival of Dancer in his favorite chair. He uttered a prayer she would safely find her way to him so he could send her after Summer.

—— oOo ——

Sunday, 3:44 p.m.

SUMMER WALKED ALONG THE streets of the town. Being late afternoon, people were making their way home from work or to the market to select food for their evening meal. She periodically looked over her shoulder to see if anyone might be following her. Every once in a while, she would catch a glimpse of the control tower at the spaceport. All she needed to do was get to the *Veritas* and this Captain Caspberry Brooks fellow, and she would be safe.

And what of this Captain Brooks? What kind of life did this starship captain have? Traveling from one planet to another with decades of suspended animation between each port of call. And then only days or weeks on planet before heading back out into space? The Old Priest said his advanced age prevented any more cycles of deep sleep.

So, this Caspberry Brooks must be a young man. Young as judged by his appearance, though. Perhaps measuring his real age in decades or even centuries might be more appropriate. Summer wondered if he flew the ship by himself. And if he did, what would it be like to live a life with no friends or family, no one special? But maybe he had a crew. And to arrive on a planet where you don't know anyone?

As the control tower loomed larger and larger, Summer thought about waking up on a new world, one on which she wouldn't know anyone. She would have to start all over again. And what about her commitment to the Church? Would this New Faith be something she could accept? Would they accept her?

And what about Dancer? Summer uttered a silent prayer her sister's plan had been successful, that she would find her way to the Old Priest, and he would send her on to the spaceport. Life on this strange new planet might just be tolerable if her sister was with her. Together they could build something.

Yes. She believed they could. *Please, dear God*, she prayed. *Keep Dancer safe.*

SIX

"It is written that 'in my Father's house are many mansions; if it were not so, I would have told you. I go to prepare a place for you.' I say to you now, this is a true statement. And that was the main purpose of my first visit to your world. Simply to say, do not fear. You will live on."
—THE CHRONICLES OF THE SECOND COMING

Sunday, 4:56 p.m.

SUMMER WAS BORN ON SOLUS II, as were her parents and her grandparents, so she had never been to the spaceport. She had watched ships take off and land as a child, but always from a distance. So, for the first time in her life, she saw a starship up close and this one was a thing of beauty. Long and silver and sleek, with three red-colored fins equally spaced around the base of the ship.

She left the terminal and walked across the tarmac, knowing her feet would, in all likelihood, never touch this world again. If she ever returned here, everyone alive today would probably be dead. Such was the price for traveling at a fraction of the speed of light and being asleep for decades with each trip.

A gangplank sloped up gently from the ground and ended at an opening in the side of the ship. Her heart felt heavy for having to leave so much behind. The monastery, her dreams of becoming one of the Sisterhood, and Dancer. Her one and only real sister. None of this would have been possible without her sacrifice.

"Welcome aboard. My name is Caspberry Brooks. I'll be your captain for the next thirty-plus years." The forty-something-year-old man gave Summer a quick wink and a slight bow before leading her to one of the sleep pods.

"If you have any possessions, you can place them in this drawer. It will seal with a biometric lock once you let it scan your fingerprint. That way, you won't forget the combination thirty years from now when you wake up."

"Just this satchel," replied Summer, feeling over-whelmed with all of the pipes and wires and equipment occupying every cubic millimeter of the ship's interior. "And, oh yes," she added. "This envelope, which I'm to assume contains payment for my passage."

The whole concept of going into a state of suspended animation for three decades? Not something she was particularly thrilled about. She sure hadn't anticipated ending her day on a sleeper ship heading out to a planet orbiting another star.

"From now on, you should not have anything to eat or drink, not even water. And anything you can do to empty your bladder and bowels would be recommended. I'll be back in an hour or so and get you settled into your sleeper pod. Until then, make yourself comfortable."

Summer looked around at the cramped quarters and tried imagining just exactly how to make herself comfortable.

The ship was certainly not built to make one feel at home. So, she found a little fold-out bench, took out the book from her satchel and started reading. As she flipped through the brittle pages, she thought about the significance of the book in her hands, about how someday in the far future, this item might become one of the most treasured relics in this New Faith, maybe even in the entire galaxy. Even though she felt as though she were giving up so much of her life for this book, it made her feel rather special, even important.

Caspberry returned after a while. Summer closed the book, kissed it, and placed it into the drawer. The computer scanned her fingerprint, and the lock on the drawer sealed with a subtle click.

She climbed into the sleep pod and felt a slight prick in her right arm as Caspberry inserted an intravenous port. He looked down at her and smiled, "Now make yourself comfortable. This is not like the old days when one had to be genetically altered before one's body could be placed into suspended animation. This will be painless and quick. Remember now, when we arrive at Vatican Prime, thirty years will have passed, and your body will need some time to adjust to being awake again. So be patient. There will be a few days between when the ship wakes you and when we land. So there's no hurry. Do you understand?"

Summer looked up at the man from her pod and mouthed the word, "Yes."

"Any other questions?"

"No."

"Okay. Get comfortable. We will be lifting off in a few hours. But you will be off in dreamland long before then. Here goes."

Caspberry sealed the pod, flicked a few switches, and watched as the purple liquid flowed down through the tube and into Summer's arm. Her eyes slowly shut, and her heart rate and respiration started to decrease.

Caspberry left Summer to her sleep and returned to the ship's entryway to greet a second passenger.

Summer never felt the tug of gravity as the ship left the spaceport and began its climb to orbit around Solus II. She had lost all awareness of her world. The chemicals the ship's computer fed her had done their work.

——— o0o ———

Thirty-plus Years Later

"GOOD MORNING, SUNSHINE," were the first words Summer heard after thirty years in a deep sleep. She had been warned waking up after being in suspended animation for so long would be difficult, even play tricks on one's mind. Somewhere deep down inside her waking mind, she knew the line between dreams and reality would be blurred.

She waited for the ship's computer to release the correct sequence of drugs through her intravenous port, drugs which would increase her metabolism, allow her organs to function at their intended levels, and clear her mind of the fog.

She started to remember things. The events at the monastery, the death of Sister Annukka, everything leading up to the need to travel to Vatican Prime. And the book. Ah, yes. The book. And the mission to deliver it to the Church on Vatican Prime. But she pushed all of those thoughts away, choosing instead to remain in her relaxed meditative state, savoring the peace for just a bit longer.

Then there was the voice again, a familiar voice. "Come on, wake up. We have a book to deliver."

Summer finally found the energy to open her eyes. A blurry image slowly came into focus. The first word she uttered as she felt her wits coming back was, "Dancer?"

POSTSCRIPT

"The message I had hoped to deliver during my first visit was simple. Do not fear. There is no need to fear death because there is no death. The body will pass away, but the soul is eternal."
—THE CHRONICLES OF THE SECOND COMING

One Year After Summer's Arrival on Vatican Prime

"SO, SISTER SUMMER, NOW THAT you've had the opportunity to read the Chronicles and meditate upon them, what do you think about their message? Did you find them enlightening?"

"I am grateful to you, Mothersoul Superior, for the chance to study the book, the book that brought me across the expanse of space to your world and to your New Faith. As I think back thirty-plus years ago to the morning that led me here, I can now understand the importance of Father Bakkar's efforts and the mission Sister Annukka gave her life to continue. And I do believe the book and the story of its origin will serve the New Faith well."

"Yes, child. But that is not an answer to my question. Did you find the text enlightening? Does the New Faith reach out to you? Does it touch your heart?"

Summer sat for a moment, then replied, "When I felt my calling to join the Sisterhood three years ago . . . sorry, that would be thirty-three years ago . . . I accepted the teachings of the New Testament and the Catholic Church as true and swore to follow our Lord and Savior, Jesus Christ. I believed in the forgiveness of sins, the resurrection of the body, and the life everlasting. Now, I'm on a new world and trying to familiarize myself with a New Faith, one that places the laws of physics in greater reverence than the grace of God. I've sacrificed so much for the sake of this New Faith, something I knew nothing about when I set foot on the sleeper ship.

"I'm grateful for the gift of the time you have given me to read, to study, and to pray about these teachings of the Second Savior. I will tell you what I think."

"Yes, go on."

"For the sake of this discussion, I will refer to the earth-centric Catholic Church as the 'Old Faith.' So, what I see is that both the Old Faith and the New Faith are very similar in so many ways. Both believe in a higher power, a power that created the universe, the many worlds humanity now lives on, and created each of us. We are the children of God. Both ask that we live our lives according to certain commandments, live in service to others, and have faith there is more beyond our earthly lives."

"Agreed," said the Mothersoul Superior.

"In assessing the faiths, I see our common reality as a house, with each faith looking into the house through different windows. Perhaps it is not so important that each of us place our faith in the validity of one window over another. Perhaps what is important is that we all place our faith in the house."

"An appropriate analogy."

"Old Earth is the birthplace for countless religions, each professing to be the one true path to a superior deity. I think it safe to say, in the end, none of these paths will prove to be entirely accurate. But I do believe there is a singular path that we will all follow once our days are over on whatever world we live. As long as we believe there is a path, I don't think the details of the path matter so much."

"I see you have given this much thought."

"So, if you are asking me, will I embrace the New Faith over the Old Faith, I can only say this. I am not certain. Maybe not now. Maybe not ever. But I am willing to live my life here on Vatican Prime with an open heart and an open mind. If the Good Lord, the Eternal Father, the One Soul, this Oversoul chooses to touch me in some way, direct me with a calling, then I will follow. I can commit to nothing more and nothing less."

"I accept everything you have said and thank you for your honesty and your commitment to serve our Higher Power, regardless of whatever name you choose to call it. And I am so grateful for the sacrifices made by you and your sister, Dancer, to deliver this most sacred of books to us here at the center of this New Faith. Without your efforts and those of Father Bakkar and Sister Annukka, our understanding of the Oversoul and how it gives life to the universe would be incomplete." The Mothersoul Superior bowed slightly to Summer as she spoke.

"As you know, I, too, have spent many days reflecting on the contents of the text written by our Second Savior and sought help from the Oversoul on how we should proceed. And notwithstanding your insightful comments, I do believe it in the best interest of the New Faith that we formally declare our intentions to break away from the Holy See, along with all of their beliefs, rituals, and Canon Law. Given it will take years for such a declaration to reach them, I have decided to make this break effective immediately rather than waiting for what will surely be decades before any response is received from the Vatican City-State on Earth.

"And I wish to clarify a point of some importance. I have sent a statement of my intentions to each of the other Outer Worlds. Naturally, it will take time for their responses to arrive back here. It will be some number of years before we might officially operate as a single body overseeing this New Faith. There is, however, one world choosing to decline our invitation to join, and that is Solus II. That is why I wanted to speak with you today. I thought you might help me understand why it is they have renewed their allegiance to the Holy See on Earth."

"Perhaps it is because of the events of three decades ago," said Summer. "Perhaps they are doing this to make some sort of amends for the loss of *The Chronicles of the Second Coming*. Perhaps they feel as though they failed in whatever mission they were given."

"I arrived at a similar conclusion," continued the Mothersoul Superior, "I have made it clear to them we will always receive them with open arms should they choose to join us as we embrace the teaching of the Second Savior.

"On a personal note, I very much regret Sister Annukka lost her life in her efforts to deliver the book to us. I pray her soul has returned to the collection of light-souls and that she knows how much we appreciate her sacrifice."

"She was a wonderful mentor," said Summer. "I do hope she knows I do not harbor any ill will toward her for involving me in her mission. It was an important mission. I understand that now."

The Mothersoul looked at Summer and offered a blessing over her.

"May the Oversoul bless you and keep you each and every day of your life."

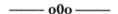

"And I will smite the winter house with the summer house; and the houses of ivory shall perish, and the great houses shall have an end, saith the Lord."

—Amos 3:15

A BIT OF BACKGROUND

TO THOSE OF YOU WHO MIGHT have read my first collection of short stories, *Seven Sides of Self*, you might notice there are more than a few connections between these new stories and some of the stories in the previous collection.

First, the planet of Aurillia was introduced in the story titled "Microwave Man." It was this same planet exosociologist, Jarka Moosha, visited in the story titled "Of The Green and Of The Gold." The beginning of that second "Aurillian Tale" describes the location of Aurillia as orbiting the star designated Lalande 21185. It just so happens the interstellar message received by Gunther Trent in "Once Upon a Helix" is from that very same planet. Knowing there is this early connection between Aurillia and Earth might help one to understand why the Aurillians had well-established "disciplines relating to extraterrestrial intelligence" (from "Of The Green and Of The Gold").

Second, Mothersouls—and the Oversoul they serve— were mentioned in both "The Ledge" and "An Intricate Balance." Their origins are explained in "The Last Sunday of Summer," and that this 'New Faith' grew out of the schism between the earth-bound Catholic Church and the more "transcendental movement centered around an

Oversoul" popping up on Earth-like exoplanets orbiting nearby stars.

Third, if one were to organize the related stories found in these two collections in a chronological manner, they would go something like this:

"Once Upon a Helix"
"The Goldfire Project"
"Half the Sky"
"Of The Green and Of The Gold"
"The Last Sunday of Summer"
"An Intricate Balance"
"The Wishbringer"
"The Ledge"

I do hope these peeks behind the curtain give you a better understanding about how "the Universe according to me" works!

NOW FOR A LITTLE BIT OF MY personal history. I transferred from the University of Maryland to Wake Forest University after my freshman year of college. It was a difficult decision, but as I look back all these years later, it was probably one of the best decisions of my life. The friends I made during those three short years have been some of my favorite people. God bless each and every one of them!

My first months at Wake Forest were tough, though. I didn't know anyone and had to start building a new social circle from scratch. But one thing that really helped was discovering something called the Experimental College. These were classes offered after hours and were for subjects one would not normally find in standard college curriculum. One of them immediately attracted my attention. It was called "Self-Actualization." The fellow teaching it was an elderly gentleman named Samuel J. Jacobson. The class, which met every Tuesday evening, was a guided meditation or a "Basic Relaxation Allowance Training Exercise." The meditations always included the mantra "perfect peace, perfect comfort, perfect health of mind, body, and spirit," the same mantra appearing in this collection's story titled "Half the Sky."

If you'd like to learn more about Sam and his guided meditation, pay a visit to: http://www.mindcontrolinamerica. com/personal-comfort-training-hypnosis-pain-relief. A hyperlink to the Personal Comfort Training is posted on the web page. Thank you so very much, Sam, for helping me through some very tough times.

raging quiet

my mind wanders
sometimes, scattering
itself amongst
the sweet and sterile
breezes by the sea.
my thoughts divide
themselves, slipping
into the dune-rills
that are shifted
and swallowed
by the breath of
many long moments.
my time gathers
together, slowly
collecting itself until
the last long minute
falls away into
the raging quiet.

december 1982
hanauma bay, oahu, hawai'i

ABOUT THE AUTHOR

NANCY JOIE WILKIE worked for over thirty years in both the biotechnology industry, and as part of the federal government's biodefense effort. She served as a project manager, providing oversight for the development of many new products.

Now retired, she composes original music, plays a variety of instruments, and is currently recording many of her compositions. She also created a series of original greeting cards displaying her artwork and photographs. Three of her prints hang on the wall at the Wake Forest University LGBTQ+ Center.

Faraway and Forever is her second collection of stories. *Seven Sides of Self* was published by She Writes Press in November 2019. A third collection of stories, titled *The River Keeper and Other Tales*, will be published in early 2024 by Austin Macauley Publishers LLC.

She resides in Brookeville, Maryland.

Author photo © Olan Mills

Creations by Nancy Joie Wilkie

Seven Sides of Self: Stories (She Writes Press, November 2019)

"Deconstructing Dad" (Pen-In-Hand, Maryland Writers' Association, January 2021)

CD—"Meditations On The Day"
(Mindsongs Musique, February 2016)

CD—"Pauper, Piper, Princes"
(Mindsongs Musique, March 2017)

CD—"Venus In The Trees"
(Mindsongs Musique, April 2019)

CD—"Aurillian Tales"
(Mindsongs Musique, June 2020)

CD—"Songs Of The Sun"
(Mindsongs Musique, December 2020)

CD—"Dragon's Door —A Tale of Ring and Sword"
(with Stephen Bloodsworth, Mindsongs Musique,
December 2022)

Greeting Cards and Prints by Mindsights Mediaworks

Produced by Nancy Joie Wilkie

CD—"The Long-Term Side Effect Soundtrack"
(by Dannie Snyder, LivCreations, 2015)

CD—"Frespirity" (by Robin Anita White,
Mindsongs Musique, May 2016)

Song—"Get Up!" (by Beyhan Çagri Trock,
Music by Beyhan, December 2017)

CD—"Three Little Words" (by Jonathan Reeve,
Mindsongs Musique, August 2021)

Visit www.mindsights.net for updates on new creations.

SELECTED TITLES FROM SHE WRITES PRESS

She Writes Press is an independent publishing company founded to serve women writers everywhere. Visit us at www.shewritespress.com.

Seven Sides Of Self: Stories by Nancy Joie Wilkie. $16.95, 978-1-63152-634-3. What would you do if you wanted something but didn't know how to get it? What if you were incarcerated but didn't know why? What if you followed up on a decades-old whim? When is a society truly perfect, and who decides? And what awaits us at the end of our lives? In this soaring short story collection, Nancy Joie Wilkie explores these questions and more.

Provectus by M. L. Stover. $16.95, 978-1-63152-115-7. A science-based thriller that explores the potential effects of climate change on human evolution, *Provectus* asks a compelling question: What if human beings were on the endangered species list—were, in fact, living right alongside our replacements—but didn't know it yet?

Life and Other Shortcomings: Stories by Corie Adjmi. $16.95, 978-1-63152-713-5. In these twelve linked short stories—pieces at once painful and yet also everyday slices of life—women and girls struggle to find their way amid cultural constraints.

Trinity Stones: The Angelorum Twelve Chronicles by LG O'Connor. $16.95, 978-1-938314-84-1. On her 27th birthday, New York investment banker Cara Collins learns that she is one of twelve chosen ones prophesied to lead a final battle between the forces of good and evil.

Time Zero by Carolyn Cohagan. $14.95, 978-1-63152-072-3. In a world where extremists have made education for girls illegal and all marriages are arranged in Manhattan, fifteen-year-old Mina Clark starts down a path of rebellion, romance, and danger that not only threatens to destroy her family's reputation but could get her killed.

The Trouble With Becoming A Witch by Amy Edwards. $16.95, 978-1-63152-405-9. Veronica thinks she's happy. But with fight after fight, night after night, she knows that something isn't right anymore. Then her husband busts her researching witchcraft—and her picturesque suburban life is turned upside down.